Praise for *Haw*

"A sort of *Brave New World* for modern times, updated with Jackson's expansive, unique vision of a world bordering on collapse, but not yet devoid of hope. The unique imagery and characters summoned in *Haw* is equal parts moving, funny, irreverent, timely, and verging on sheer brilliance. I relished every moment of it."

—Mitch Cullin, author, *Tideland*

"Haw ventures into dystopiana with cli-fi aplomb. A novel worth savoring."

—Dan Bloom, *The Cli-Fi Report*

"Kept me on the edge of my seat"

—*LitPick,* 5-Star Review

Haw

by

Sean Jackson

Harvard Square Editions
New York
2015

Published in the United States by
Harvard Square Editions

ISBN: 978-1-941861-06-6

Harvard Square Editions web address:
www.HarvardSquareEditions.org

Printed in the United States of America

Haw is a work of fiction. Names, characters, businesses,
places, events and incidents are either the products of the
author's imagination or used in a fictitious manner. Any
resemblance to actual persons, living or dead, or actual events
is purely coincidental.

1.

THE COLD SEIZES LUCAS as he steps off the train into a bitter brew of sleet and mud. The wet air leeches through his jacket and shoes as he joins a throng of *citoyens*, pushing through a wall of them, clothed in fetid rags, as they grunt along the platform, a horde of savages staggering in a hundred directions home.

All he can think about is water. He's seen rusty tanks and leaky lines, the stagnant reservoir ponds choked with bacteria. Lucas knows the hardships facing his efforts to find enough velocity to scour the city pipes clean to protect the city's fragile supply of drinking water. It's a losing battle. Some are saying it's already lost.

There have been nine deaths in the past week due to high levels of Legionella. Nine that were reported. He knows the count is higher, that bodies stay wrapped in rancid quilts all winter since most families are frightened of the cost to bury their dead. Or else they are simply too far gone to take care of it themselves.

And if the water degrades further, it could mean the collapse of the nuclear reactor. The nuke is all that keeps central North Carolina valuable to the government. Without it, civilization here would end—like it has ended elsewhere in the country. Lucas has seen those darkened places, the Deep South and the West. Like collapsed stars gasping for air.

Lucas skids a bit in the muck, edging his way through a pack of youths huddled against a fence. He is a thin, ordinary man who tries to evade confrontations. He turns his small, square jaw toward the youths. Some of these young never seem to go home. They are always gathered here, burning castoffs to stay warm on the street. A rat-faced blonde boy pokes his tongue out at Lucas, screws his eyes, and makes an obscene gesture, all to the delight of his pack.

Tainted water, which has afflicted the population for decades now, has produced decrepit boys like this one.

Pollutants are to blame for the hordes of citoyens who do little more than smear their presence on history, like feces on a public toilet wall.

"Bubbly ho!" the boy says with a grimace, and then urinates on Lucas's shoes.

There is so much water that is contaminated for so much of its course up through the bedrock, that Water Purification has about given up on achieving sanitary levels. As Lucas sees his house, where his son Orel is making supper, he mentally notes the final number of the week: fifty-four percent. Even rounded up, that's devastatingly low—borderline toxic. And that was their best drinking water of the week.

It takes him a moment to unlock the front door, the sizzling entry light an orange glow on his hands, then the warmth in the foyer like a gust from an oven. He calls out to his son as he hangs his jacket. There is music from the kitchen. The boy is playing the old records, one of the scratchy vinyls that bellow from the jazz age.

"Need help?" Lucas asks. Orel is stirring at the stove, dodging columns of steam from a big pot. His hands are strong, his arms sinewy, and he stands like a boxer with a towel draped over his shoulder. The boy has been doing much of the cooking since his mother died.

"Naw," Orel says. "I've got it under control. Just go ahead and sit if you want to. I'll have it ready in a minute."

Egg noodles and strands of fried pork. This is their Friday meal. Humble, sufficiently nourishing, and accompanied by jazz or some Baroque strings, with a bottle of old, cheap wine. Lucas wants them to celebrate making it through each week without falling sick or being hit in the head by one of the drifters. Orel has just turned sixteen. He made it through the womb and birth without neurological disorder. He has grown up normal. His photography proves he is of sound mind. Orel's pictures are printed and framed all over the walls, upstairs and downstairs.

"Are we going to the market this weekend?" Orel asks at the table, as his father comes to the end of a red Appalachian port wine.

If the sleet turns to snow, which is possible this early in March, they cannot walk to the market. That would mean riding the buses, which can be unreliable, but they could use the time together.

"Sure," Lucas says. "Why not?"

The windows are fully dark. The music still plays. There is nothing left on their plates but clay-colored stains from the meal. Nothing goes to waste. Lucas wonders how much longer they can keep on like this. If the government doesn't cut off his work benefits, then this anxiety or exhaustion could put an end to it. It seems the boy may be tiring, given the growing demands of living in a dying city. The strain of it saps him more and more. When Orel was little, just after Sila died, Lucas worried about him all the time. He still worries. He fears what would happen to Orel if he died, with the mother already gone.

"I want to get things to make a cake," Orel says. "I never got that cake for my birthday."

The milk is sketchy, but there is synthetic butter. It is mostly the water they have to fear, but the air is polluted. People still say, "The sky is making our children stupid." There are people who haven't come out of their homes for years. These are mostly wealthy people, who live downtown in the old industrial sections, the tall buildings and the condos, where police protection is heavy. These are not the citoyens. They are the Hidden.

The Hidden have secured their safety due to wealth, through generations of hoarding money and accumulating the power that goes with it. They sleep peacefully, in controlled climates, away from the writhing violence and poverty that has wrecked the citoyens. Across the country, tens of thousands— compared to millions of citoyens—are secluded in virtual fortresses. There are those who predict the world will come full circle, eventually staggering to a bloated death, once the brute force of nature realizes how far gone it is. The Hidden have plundered natural resources to survive in their towers. Entire economies have been kicked over to secure this unholy imbalance. There are those who say the time is soon coming for the pendulum to swing back.

"So?" Orel says, breaking his father's daydream. "The cake?"

"You bet. We can make it more than one layer. And red velvet—sort of a red velvet. You can fake it the best you can. At least it'll be red. You can use a little wine if you have to. The alcohol will cook out."

Orel smiles. He has just started shaving, but his face still looks like a boy's. The skin shines softly, the eyes bright, and the hair always crew cut. Very healthy. Quite brilliant. Lucas could not be more proud.

He knows they have it better than so many others, namely the citoyens who are apparently genetically programmed to suffer. Some people claim the citoyens are bred to absorb the wastes of this world. In his darker moments, Lucas thinks that somebody, like his current boss, Gail, needs to figure out what to do with them. Gail is the head of the city's Public Vita, a collective of divisions and forces that oversee water and transportation, in addition to the darker elements of the government—military and resource control. Gail's power is deep and far-reaching.

Lucas is a scientist in Water Purification, one of the worst places to work. There is never any good news, nor any victories against pollution. The turnover rate is high, especially given the lurking, sinister presence of government overseers like Gail. But Lucas has Orel to keep his thoughts from getting too bleak. There are those who having nothing and nobody else besides the lure of staying on, staying the course, until the time comes when they join the Hidden.

"I have to go to the school next week," Orel says, as he draws back stiffly in his chair. His blue eyes drift to the nearest window, where he can see the lights from surrounding houses blaze in all varieties of colors, and smoke drifts innocuously pale and calm from dozens of chimneys. "I have to take my last exam in front of a public academic."

Lucas knows Orel hates this. The boys used to taunt him mercilessly. The girls too. So many of his classmates were damaged in their brains, if not their hearts and souls. The schools are not safe, and they teach the children nothing. The only good, kind students have left the schools to study at home, as Orel did when he turned fourteen.

"I can take off work and come with you," Lucas says.

Orel shakes his head. "I don't care about them anymore," he says, dragging his fork through a greasy stain on his plate. "I haven't cared about them in a long time." In fact, he hasn't cared about his former friends and classmates ever since nobody came to see him after the last time he was beaten almost three years ago. Added to all the other assaults and insults, that particular beating was the catalyst for moving forward with homeschooling. After all, the police don't do anything they don't want to do. Orel was beaten outside the schoolyard by a circle of lazy-eyed citoyen offspring because he had drawn a picture of a young boy—no older than him—wearing female clothing. It was very Greek and androgynous. It was an example of his artistic talents.

Those goons, which is an old term Lucas draws upon to refer to those youths who exhibit a moral vacuum, fractured Orel's skull and cracked one of his legs, leaving him terrified of ever returning to school, or even leaving the house. His spirit was broken for a long time.

But Orel is bigger now. And he is not afraid. Things around the city have grown so much worse over such a short period of time. The idea of hope, of positivity in general, has been consumed by a bleak and overarching pessimism that people are calling a numbness.

"A lot of them are sick," Orel says of his attackers, past enemies. "Or dead."

"Still," Lucas says gently, stretching in his chair.

There is plenty of night left, but they do not go out. It's difficult to gauge what it would be like out there. Crime is always in flux, but of late it is spiking terribly. Lucas hears that the root cause of it is in their lungs. The very air that they breathe is growing worse by the day, just like the water that Lucas and his colleagues allow to course through the pipes into homes and buildings. At night, in this late-winter season, the air hangs thick with contaminants.

An Air Quality guy had been going around saying that this was the end, that the ecosystems were doomed. He pinned

Lucas to the wall of an elevator one morning and ranted about thresholds, saying they'd all been breached. The guy looked awful, like he'd just come out of a nightmare. And then he disappeared, nowhere to be seen. That was maybe two weeks ago, and the air has turned worse since then. It reeks. The water numbers are tumbling, too, and Lucas is afraid that this is an irreversible trend. But water has been a problem for decades. This spoiled air—it speaks to a far greater problem. People can boil water, in most cases, to make it safe. But there's no getting around breathing. A person can't just substitute this or that for oxygen.

So Lucas hates to go out at all. It has been so bad lately that Lucas and Orel haven't been out together at night. Between the violence and the weather, they only go out in the day, and then only when it is necessary.

"Let's go upstairs," Lucas says, deciding not to do the dishes. It's a whole ordeal, because of the water. "I want to see what you've been working on this week."

They use a lighted rear stairwell that spirals up. Their house, when it was built fifty years before, was for a large, affluent family who apparently admired Italianate design. There are balconies all around the upstairs, ornate corbels fastened everywhere. It's painted a sunny peach (a "virginal blush" Lucas has heard it called), and the ceilings are high and grand, with stunning details. Five decades before, this neighborhood—in the suburbs, to the west of the city—was still in its prime. You had to be somebody to live here. You owned lots of dogs, hired gardeners, stocked the wine cellar, all of that.

The difference now is almost unbelievable. Before the newspapers stopped printing, they wrote about places like this, how these enormous villas were being vacated by their wealthy owners so that the owners could seek refuge and hiding in downtown skyrises, where the police and military protection could be bought.

Lucas moved them in when it became just him and Orel. Somebody at work had spoken of the place, tucked safely within a hive of mansions, where everything was still functioning and clean. There was a deposit, and that was all.

No rent. Definitely no mortgage. And while others pay steep water and electric rates, Lucas gets free utilities, because he works for the government. This allows him to commute into the city by train for work, which would otherwise be a financial burden. It has allowed him and Orel to eat well, and take precautions for their safety.

But these perks are starting to pale, with food and income becoming an afterthought to the growing violence and unrest throughout the city. What good does it do to have a bottle of wine and a good meal, Lucas thinks, when someone is soon to slit your throat?

Nowadays, their neighbors are a mixture of lowlifes and recluses. This wet winter is hard on many. The deaths are rising. People are scared. He saw a young mother last week, by the public bank, begging for someone to buy her child. The poor baby was dead, and she knew it. She advertised it as a little corpse that could at least feed some animals, perhaps even an indiscriminate sibling or two.

The woman smoked as she stood by the corner of the building, a boxy brick and glass job with accountants and clerks huddled inside. The sun streaked under approaching afternoon clouds and bathed her in its fleeting light. Her dirty fur coat flapped in the wind and her hands bled from exposure. She told passerby the baby's name was Shane and that it had enjoyed a good upbringing, at least for a time.

Lucas found the nerve to step over and ask how her child died, since he wanted to make at least a little donation to her cause, whatever it might be.

"It's not my baby," the woman said. "I found it."

There is a lot of this, this sort of wading through facts, facades, petty crimes and vulgar magic tricks. This was one of the worst Lucas had run into. Not too long ago, he would have alerted the authorities about this atrocity, and they would have responded swiftly. But now people go to such lengths to flaunt the lawlessness in the city, he knows better.

The woman poked her gloved fingers into the baby's face, which was gray as iron.

"It doesn't have eyes," she said wistfully, then looked up at him. "It wasn't born with eyes."

2.

Lucas made only one trip since the death of his wife, a viewing of wastelands in the South and West. He traveled with a team, a quintet of sleep-deprived government officials tasked with figuring out how to keep blight from crawling up the East Coast and infecting the major cities.

They rolled along in a military tracker. Lucas was quiet and window-gazing, while the others rattled off stories of visits to the Gulf, the colorful deserts, open ranges, all the places since wrecked by waves of privation and war.

They sped into the bayous, where citoyens lined the highways pleading for a ride out. The driver explained that this was due to cholera, undrinkable water, and lawless tribes who had reverted to primitive ways in order to survive. These wild faces were new to Lucas then, some were even violently sunburned (he would never see *that* again), and others were just desperate, filthy, their bodies swollen from improper diets. The team drove straight to a line of old Spanish houses—a plantation—where they met with grim-faced officials who spoke in hushed tones about the state of things.

As the sun set in the old warped windows, Lucas heard of inoperable sewer systems, sediment-choked flow pipes, and general malaise that was now quickly turning into chaos. There was no food being trucked in. The tribes were burning entire housing complexes and the state government had been removed "as you would a dead tooth."

The picture only got uglier. They saw corpses floating in swamp canals. They witnessed the execution of a tribal leader, with a rag over his face, crumpling to the ground as they shot him. A meeting with a local man, a former mayor of a local parish, provided only a soliloquy of tears and reprimands, until the man was eventually dragged out screaming.

A tiny, arthritic old Cajun came in during one dinner and told how spillways were flooded, dams were bulldozed, and retaining ponds for the oil industry and power companies had been emptied out into rivers and lakes. What needed to end, came to an end.

"Our way of life is done," the old Cajun lamented. "Time for us to move on."

The caravan also moved on, northwest into the Great Plains—a vast, arid field of ghosts and brush fires. The smoke was so thick it was hard to see the ruins. The driver gave accounts of abandoned ranches, the air so toxic that you couldn't even breathe in a basement with piped-in oxygen. The fires were out of control. They would rage into the Rockies, jumping rivers, until the ever-present rains of later years would put them out, yielding a cauterized landscape.

They went into Utah, then Nevada, to look at old America and the travesty of "resource conservation." The term, as it was explained to them, meant depriving one area of its protective efforts (irrigation, firefighters, highway maintenance, public water, etc.) to support another area deemed more capable of survival. By that time, the bottom two-thirds of the country was in full deprivation.

"Never mind the lost resources," the driver said. "Population shrinkage should coincide with that, so that they move in tandem. Remember the dead tooth analogy?"

It was simple enough to understand: the government was sacrificing many to save a few. Slowly, the territories deemed worthy of surviving were being clustered around epicenters of the powerful and wealthy, within cities. Lucas could not sleep at night. He sensed the imbalance—impoverished multitudes scavenging the outlying, rural wastes ... set against the weaponized, monetized urban minority—couldn't hold its weight forever. What if the citoyens eventually rebelled? And, even worse, what if the uprising was strong? Would the government sabotage its only refuge, the cities? All of this weighed on his mind, worried him that the world may not endure long enough for Orel to grow old.

His button, despite its being a proper government device, rarely got a signal, and he had gone days without contact with his son. There was no news of home, which Lucas now saw as a place more vulnerable than ever. Out here, everything had been ravaged for decades, and inconsistent planning and efforts to control abuse were identical to what he saw just starting to take shape in the East. The only difference was the availability of water, the proximity of oceans, rivers and lakes—and those who had proximity, had a chance to survive. As long as the waters held up, were kept clean enough to support power stations, nukes and drinking supplies, the shoreline and lakeside lands would maintain.

But these dusty sprawls and echo canyons were doomed from the start. In a town where casinos used to attract drunken, cash-flush tourists, a crowd of rail-thin citoyens stood in the weedy parking lot of a motel. They were barbecuing dogs.

"Look at that," the driver said.

They pulled right up against the curb and watched. Nobody spoke. The driver fiddled with his button, not even bothering to look. He finally asked the scientists: "What do you see?" The motel parking lot had a dozen languid forms huddled around a can fire, with a couple of them chewing on charred meat at any given moment. They could not be seen clearly and showed no interest in the military vehicle. Most of them were naked or in rags.

"Nobody," the driver said. And then, wholly unconcerned, he rolled down his window and fired a pistol into the crowd. And then he drove off.

That night they camped in a cold canyon under a clear sky. It was the first view unobscured by clouds or smoke in days. They built a fire and ate from ration cans, which made the driver laugh. He seemed to be growing more unhinged the longer they stayed on the road. He had not shaved since they crossed the Mississippi. He started making his calls in secret, so they couldn't hear any of what was being said. One of the men claimed he had seen the driver praying, in secret, back in Kansas. He'd gone behind another truck, gotten on one knee, and put his hands together and closed his eyes.

"He wasn't praying to God", Lucas said, weary of this trip and ready to be firmly on the path home. "Probably he was praying to his superior officer, or for someone to kill us."

They all had their first laugh in days. They talked about what it was they were supposed to be getting from this trip.

The plan was for them to draft solutions for saving the failing water and air supplies by seeing how systems had failed. But it didn't seem to be producing any data or providing much useful information, other than to see what a horrid landscape the U.S. was becoming.

From the scarce news that got in, they knew that the rest of the world was no better off. There were pockets of relief from the horrors of toxic water, starvation, violence and disturbing greed—and they were rumored to lay only in coastal Asia and much of Australia. The mountains of Europe were in tatters and the entire continent of Africa was deserted, save for secretive military expeditions. America was falling with the rest of the world, perhaps even faster.

As they turned back east, they learned that one of the men's wives had fallen ill. The driver heard of this and quietly lit a cigarette and gave it some thought.

"You want me to drive faster or something," he asked the man with the sick wife. They were stopped outside the gates of a small military base in the Ozarks, roughly the divide between devastation and civilization.

"Do you think if I drive really fast you can make it home before she dies?"

The man with the sick wife explained that she was gravely ill but not presently dying.

The driver responded with a grumble, "then what is the big freaking hurry?" He went in the truck, locked the doors, and got on his button.

The men gathered off to the side, where a nest of highway signs shielded them from the driver's view. Lucas got on his button and reached Orel for the first time in a week. He nearly wept as the boy told him mundane things that were happening in school, and about the place where he was staying.

"Dad?"

"Yes, Son."

"Are you okay?"

"Sure. Sure I am." And he would wait years before telling Orel what he saw out there, the suffering and wasting away of so much, of everything it seemed. What use would he have in telling him?

"I'll be there to get you tomorrow, late, and I will take you home."

Lucas wiped his eyes and heard the driver climb out of the truck. He said goodbye to Orel. The driver stomped over. The man's face was red with anger. He said they would be driving all night in order to get back into North Carolina ahead of schedule. He made a point of saying it was not due to the sick wife. Rather, it was because of something that mattered. He looked at Lucas.

"Your boss, Gail, says to call him immediately. Says you've got his new number, if you just check in on your messages and call the first chance you get, which means now."

They drove into the Smokies before stopping again. The truck had a bad tire that had to be switched out. That gave them an hour or so to stretch and eat before the last blast into Raleigh.

Lucas joined the others at a shabby little restaurant just up the grade from where they'd broken down. The driver stayed with the truck, cursing and chain smoking. He hadn't slept in nearly twenty-four hours. The sun would soon come up.

The restaurant had a few people in it. There were two occupied tables under some blacked-out windows with weary couples who looked as if they had been out working in the forests for a long time. They watched the men come in, sipped their coffee without speaking, and finally shifted their gazes back to each other.

Lucas and his group fell into a booth on the far side and ordered coffee and eggs with waffles, toast, fruit and pastries— everything the cooks in the back could make. They had a payment card the driver had given them. They talked excitedly and waited for their food.

But when it came, it was like someone had died. The plates looked horrible, as though children had cooked for the first time. The eggs (powdered) were an awful orange, the waffles were scorched, and the fruit was obviously past its date, all shriveled and soft. The people at the other tables laughed softly.

The man with the sick wife cut his eyes at them. By this time, he was sleepless with concern about his wife. He was at a tipping point. He ran his hand through his graying hair and banged on the table. The dirty forestry couples only laughed harder. The men were young and muscled underneath damp sweaters and vests. They wore beards and wool caps. The women dressed the same and also had mud and debris caked onto their clothing.

The man with the sick wife looked over and called out an insult. He stood up and bared his teeth and pointed at the closest young man. He said it was a shame that some people have it so good. He threatened to call in their psychotic driver to shoot these people.

The young couples just stared. They looked at each other again, then back to the booth. They laughed harder than before. One of the men took off his cap, spit in it, and flung it at the yelling man whose wife was (unknown to him) dying of a fever.

Lucas had to grab his new friend by the shoulders and shove him back into the booth. The man was shaking, demanding to be let go. It took three of them to get this average-sized scientist under control. When they finally had him subdued, he broke into sobs, his hands over his face and his elbows digging around in his crappy food on the table until a saucer and mug crashed to the floor.

Lucas forgot the other table. He helped his friend up and half-carried him to the door. It was drizzling outside and they slow-walked toward the truck, a quarter-mile off.

"I can't do this anymore," the friend told Lucas. He said it was not a world he could deal with. The only thing keeping him going was his wife. Then he stopped and leaned against a highway marker and checked his button. Lucas was eyeing the truck (the driver was nowhere to be seen) when his friend howled and took off running down the road. He ran straight into an oncoming semi. Blood splatters flew far enough to fleck Lucas's cheeks.

* * *

There is a nutty smell to the rooms in the school, almost like peanut butter. Orel has come to the school to take his exit exam, hoping that this will carry him a stride closer to his goal of moving on to a university in the North. It is better up there in many ways. The water is still drinkable; the air doesn't make people so sick.

Walking quickly down the bright hallway, Orel notices school is over for the day. Many days now are just half days. There are a few straggling teachers gathering papers in their rooms, and somebody is talking loudly on a button—and smoking—in the lounge. Orel listens to this as he heads for the cafeteria, where a handful of homeschoolers will take their exam.

The smoker is haggling over a delivery of something, trying to make hay of someone's demise down the line. He laughs. Orel moves farther away, almost to the cafeteria doors now.

Eyes rise from low-slung tables as he comes in. Most of them are peering into tablets, swiping and sending, waiting for the test to begin.

"All buttons up front," the proctor—a gaunt, disheveled man Orel remembers haunted the science rooms upstairs—says. But Orel does not bring his phone out with him. He is tired of having goons steal his button.

None of the kids are passing up their phones. They sneak them into pockets or packs and stare blankly at the proctor. Orel remembers the man a little more, every time he delves into his clouded memory of going to school here. It was just one awful year, chaotic and scarring. And this thin, nervous old man used to scurry around, darting his wet eyes at students, making this wheezing sound as he went.

"You can begin," says the proctor, who is still making this sound as he passes out exam sheets to each of the homeschoolers. "Let me know when you are finished. There will be no cheating."

Orel zeros in on this man, a curious and cold type who perceives that this world is populated exclusively by cheaters and schemers. Which is mostly true, Orel admits to himself as the proctor (*Mr. What? Mr. Who? … what is his name!*) smacks his test on the table and wheezes. Orel understands the impulse the cheat, the *need* of it. There are few ways out for those in the middle, people without wealth or strong government connections. They are being squeezed thin, and if you don't rise up, you plummet.

"Cheating will be punished," the old professor snorts as he returns to the front of the room. "Severely, swiftly, and in totality. Now, good luck on your examinations."

The man sits and opens a book as Orel and the others begin filling in ovals with lead pencils. You could easily cheat, Orel sees. This proctor tucks his face deep within his book and all you can see are his gnarled fingers wrapping around the edges. He is reading a book of philosophy and laughs softly to himself, dog-earing pages as he goes. One of the girls carefully extracts her tablet from a bag on the floor, powers up, and starts researching answers.

It goes on like this for two hours. Rain and sleet begin to pelt the windows along the back of the room. It becomes a steady, cozy drumming that soothes the distressed minds of the teenagers hunched over their exams. Orel's own anxiety diminishes as he nears the end and stretches out a bit, letting blood run back into his feet.

The old proctor looks up from his compendium of moral habits, and he frowns. He removes his wire glasses and rubs his eyes, a childlike movement, until someone giggles. And before long there are several of them laughing softly. The man returns his glasses to his nose and yawns as he raises the book back up so that it shields his face.

"Last hour," he says from behind his book.

But Orel is finished. He lays his pages in front of the proctor and scrawls his signature on the list. He isn't the first to go, but he is close. He looks back up to the skylights as he retraces his way down the hall. It's not dark yet, but the sky has become an evil blue-gray. As a photographer, the color is mesmerizing. But for someone who is about to step out into the weather, it is boilerplate ominous.

"Hello," a haggard woman by the school fence says to him, as he makes his way down the street. She is seated on a low stone bench that Orel remembers as a place where the freshmen girls camped out, sniggering and taunting younger boys, fat girls, anyone with mental issues.

Orel smiles at the woman and keeps walking. She flicks her cigarette at his feet to get his attention. When he turns, she is coughing wildly into her palm, where phlegm is collecting at an alarming rate.

"Hey," she sputters. "You can buy my baby?"

She points to a wad of soiled fabric at her feet. Orel just turns and goes. There is no need to find out what is going on. You never will, in a situation like this. That person will just keep weaving fantasy after fantasy until you're exhausted with it, and you either hit her across the face or, in this case, buy her baby.

"It was raised proper," the citoyen woman calls after him, "for a time."

He has to wrap his head with a leather scarf as he goes down the hill for the first leg of the labyrinth of streets and boulevards home. The ice has begun to catch in his short hair and cling to his temples, anything that is exposed. He can't ride the bus because he couldn't find his pass. Besides, the bus is teeming with perverts and oddities, like the woman selling her dead baby outside the school, seeking shelter from the elements. He has had his fill of the nearly dead on the bus. And it doesn't really save him much time with the route it takes, meandering from one vicinage to another like it is lost, stopping whenever the driver feels that he needs to roll to the curb and drink vodka from his cup.

Orel likes to run a good deal of the way home. It keeps him in shape, and nobody bothers a runner. But today that is out of the question, as there is just too much ice on the ground to navigate. So he leaves a slit to see through the scarf and trots when he can, whenever the steam from sewers or manholes gouges a raw swath of slippery mud through the icy terrain. He recalls how these neighborhoods, not so long before, were decent sprawling neighborhoods with clean yards, and cars in their garages. There used to be other kids to play with around here, just blocks from his home. There was a little redhead boy, who was crazy about riding bicycles and even jumping small ramps with flames (caused by pouring lighter fluid in the dead grass) licking up along the runway.

But the little redhead did not grow up to be big and strong and useful and smart, like Orel has done. The little redhead was recruited by the labs for testing, and simply vanished one day, never to reappear on his bike, pedaling crazily toward the flame-raked ramp. There were others like this, and the last of Orel's sane and able-bodied friends joined the military over the past couple of years. They wanted the safety and the career tenure offered, even if travel was no longer an option. The brightest of his friends were lucky enough to get into universities.

Orel has been relatively alone for some time now. He holes up in his room and reads anything he can get his hands on. His father has a quasi-library, mostly books from Orel's grandparents, plus a few picked up along the way. A lot of their books were lost in the fire. Most everything they had at the time was lost in the fire, including Orel's mother, Sila.

"Hey," Orel calls as he approaches the house and sees a feral-looking kid shaking something out of their trash.

"Mind your own business," the kid snarls, keeping his back to Orel. He is removing anything that is made of plastic from the trashcans. There is a pile of it at his feet, glazed with sleet and ice. Scavengers can still get a little money from the state when they carry plastic to the recycling plant. But they have to get all the way out there, and word is that the cash payments for recyclables will soon end. Lucas says there isn't enough good water left to be wasting it on the recycling processes.

Orel unwinds his scarf and drifts away a little, into the yard, to sit under an arbor (where vines of wisteria still remain, though in tatters) and watch this kid scavenge to his heart's content. The ice spatters the arbor's wood beams, producing a mist of sleet, as Orel watches the kid. When the pile is knee high, the kid extracts a black polythene bag from his pants and begins shoving in the plastic. He is like a comedic Santa when he is done, as he hefts the sack over his shoulder and trudges off, bowlegged and purposeful.

Orel uses his keys to get in the front door, a system of half a dozen locks and slide bolts. He brings up the fire before heading into the kitchen to start dinner.

* * *

They keep a fire going for as much of the year as they can, to keep the flies out of the house. It works wonders until the summer months, when it is still far too hot to have the fireplaces going. That's when people buy birds and lizards and whatever will eat insects out of the air. Every year, as the gloom thickens, the bugs grow worse. As a result, there is good money to be had in the pet bird and lizard market, and a fair number of their neighbors make a living raising midge-eaters.

Orel often jokes to his father that what they are having for dinner is a finch or an iguana. A lot of what they buy at the market could be mistaken for small birds or reptiles, as far as their proteins are concerned.

"My great-grandfather used to raise chickens," Lucas sometimes likes to boast during meals, when he has an excess of wine. "He kept them in long, heated houses, in rows like tin apartment houses, and they always had the lights on inside because chickens love to read."

Even the first time he heard this, Orel was skeptical.

"You can't raise chickens like that," he said. "You can only raise them underground."

Lucas waved him off.

"Before the air was bad, you could do a lot of things we can't do now."

"I know, Dad. You could have a county fair and acrobats in a circus, all out in the great wide-open spaces of America and Mother Earth. I just didn't realize they could do chickens is all."

"Literary chickens."

"Of course. Dickens' chickens."

Orel cooks with a lot of salt and wild onions, since their food would be otherwise bland. They sometimes drink hot teas (boiled for prolonged periods and spiked with chlorine tablets). Nobody has perfected the mass cleansing ritual for colas, and definitely not for milk. Not even almond or soy milks. It's hard on infants. The few who get through infancy without disorders and birth defects are, the way Orel sees it, not as lucky as his father thinks. Perhaps it is easier to have attention deficit disorder or to be on the autism spectrum, because then you may not fully realize the despair that awaits you, should you have a long life.

Orel argued this point with his father earlier in the week. As usual, Lucas tried to persuade his son to see the practical side: modern life offers few escapes. Finally, Orel gave in to despair.

"Have you ever thought it? Have you ever thought maybe we'd be better off dead?

Lucas had thought it, and yet it was one lie he didn't mind telling his son.

"Never," he said. "But I would give my life for you. I couldn't die in your mother's place, but I would die in yours."

* * *

Their closest neighbor is a philosopher who has shut himself in as he waits to join the Hidden in the city. He lectured at the university downtown. The professor is Hungarian and plays beautiful piano and paints abstracts. He was a smiling presence until his wife ran off and his children vowed never to set foot in America again.

The man's face is a weaving of vertical slags of skin and cholesterol deposits, from which brown eyes beam, sharp as points. The professor never combs his hair and was called Einstein or Beethoven, depending upon the disposition of his students. They can still hear his Steinway breezing through a famous sonata, climbing the arpeggios frantically, or simmering down, woefully, until the soft chords become whispers.

Orel has seen his father cry secretly, when their neighbor plays late at night during a snowfall. It is as if the two men are communicating. The more Lucas weeps the more melancholy the music becomes.

"I don't want the professor to leave," Orel says, "even if he does make you sad."

Lucas refrains from saying how dangerous it will become in this neighborhood soon enough. When the pollutants abate in the summer, and maybe some new clean water is found, the crime will spike again. The old professor knows he would not survive another round of wildings and raids and burglaries. It was during the last peak of violence that someone set Lucas's house on fire. And that was in a secure neighborhood. But it turned quickly. They had been making plans to leave when Sila stayed home to work one day, with Lucas at work and Orel in school. She never had a chance. She burned alive, one of several that day, the gloomy sky lit orange with burning homes.

"Everyone who can leave should do it," Lucas tells his son every time the subject of the professor leaving comes up. "There is absolutely no reason to wait. Do you remember how your mother would say it would eventually be our time to pack up and leave for the skyrises?"

Orel doesn't remember. He wonders if his mother ever said such a thing at all.

"'Sila,' I would say, 'we have plenty of time. We can wait. What's the worst that can happen?'"

Lucas grows dejected when he says this, on the night after Orel's exam, and he clutches a bottle of burgundy tightly to his chest. They sit on a divan in front of the fire in the library. It is snowing, and the professor is full bore at his Steinway, carving his path through Bach's *Passions*.

"You should stop drinking so much wine," Orel says, holding his button out so his father can see a picture he's just snapped. "It turns your teeth red. See?"

Lucas turns bleary eyes to his son. It is too hard for him to tell, despite the glowing screen. He goes back to staring into the firebox, wondering who carved the griffins that guard the marble flanks and cause shadows to dance upon the walls to the left and right.

"What's the worst thing that can happen?" he mutters.

Orel looks at his father, sees the man's sad eyes are nearly closed, his chin digging into his chest.

"Well," Orel says, "you should at least think about your liver."

* * *

Lucas is shoveling the walkway in the morning, the sky still heavy and ashen, when Orel comes around the side of the house, between a pair of dead shrubs.

"He's moving out right now," Orel says. "There is a truck backed up to his house and they just put his piano in. He's out in the yard in his pajamas, waving at the moving men like a maniac, and singing at the top of his lungs."

"I hear him," Lucas says, still shoveling.

"Don't you want to say goodbye, Dad?"

"No need," Lucas says.

Orel shrugs and goes over to watch. The men lugging out their neighbor's things are bearded muscular types, like Vikings, who wear fur-cuffed boots and long chains around their necks. They speak in a foreign language and pay no attention to the animated professor, who is red-faced in anger over something they have done.

"Isten, légy irgalmas nekem, bűnösnek!" the professor yells, thrusting a champagne bottle into the air. On and on, he rants, until one of the movers kicks snow at him. Orel moves closer, so close he can smell the rich cigar smoke on the Vikings. They are hefting furniture and boxes that would snap any normal man's tendons, rip the muscles right from the bone.

"What is he saying to you?" Orel asks one of the movers, who is smiling. The man displays his big ugly teeth and glares mirthfully right into the boy's eyes.

"He says, 'God, have mercy on me, a sinner,'" the Viking says, laughing. "And it is true. He sins in ways you and I have never thought of."

The professor whirls around and laughs, drinking hungrily from his magnum. He salutes Orel and does a silly dance in the snow.

"Isten, légy irgalmas nekem, bűnösnek!" the professor cries out, sending them all into laughter.

3.

Shrouding itself in bureaucracy and cynicism, the government continually fails to be responsible to its people, Tainted water is a by-product of government dysfunction, producing generations of beastly people—the citoyens. They cleave their way through life without the means to eat proper food, wear adequate clothing, or even live in sanitary and safe homes. They have a medieval existence, as a result of horrid governing, economic corruption, endless wars, and contaminated water.

There was a day recently when the lake reservoir overflowed its banks, submerging a city of huts along the river downstream. There was nothing unusual about that. The lake was engineered nearly a century before and was never expected to handle the inflows it received. These huts were built on pilings that raise them out of the muck, above the debris from these frequent floods. But when the water receded, this time it was different.

A new form of squalor invaded the hut city. There were deadly gases this time, smoking up from the river. An eerie glow was reported. People foamed at the mouth and bled from their eyes. A child was brought into the city, alone in the back of an armored truck, with involuntary shaking, blinding seizures, and black vomit that smelled like turpentine.

He went to a building not far from Lucas's office. Lucas went down to try to get an understanding of what was going on. A soldier hosed out the truck used to transport the boy, and Lucas stopped to ask him about the boy and the swamped hut city.

"It ain't the flu," the soldier, a middle-aged and heavyset Southerner, told him. "I can tell you that, and that is all I can tell you. It definitely ain't the flu."

By the end of the week the boy was forgotten, and Water Purification was desperately trying to sort out the cause of other deaths, blackouts, and fits that had sent people to the asylums. This wasn't just a case of pollution, Lucas told a colleague. It was bigger, more volatile, excessively noxious, and left a swath of death like no other he had seen in his twenty years working for the government.

"What do you think it is?" his colleague asked.

He said he didn't know. That was the problem. He just didn't know, and nobody else seemed to know either, not even enough to venture a guess.

"The only clear-cut data I have," he said ruefully, "is that it is not the flu virus."

In all, seventy people died, including the boy and his entire family. Lucas heard the hut city was intentionally burned out, slathered in oily tar and set on fire, and the military came in to prevent anyone from coming back. A friend of his at Transportation said a different theory floated through his office: there was a toxic discharge from the nuclear plant.

"But that's downstream," Lucas said. They were having lunch in the atrium of a once-bustling legislative complex, where government workers have meals and sleep on cots when they cannot—or do not want to—ride the train home.

"Not even a government watershed anymore," Lucas added.

His friend, Juda, a half-Pakistani with immaculate hands, winked. He looked carefully around the gloomy hall, as if wanting to share a prized secret with Lucas.

"'Anymore' is the key word here," Juda whispered. "We've sent boxcars to that area of late, hundreds of them, and more tractor trailers than I thought we even had in our fleet. Like some kind of migration. But I don't really know if it's going in or out—an exodus or a pilgrimage. Either way, something important is happening out there. But I don't know if it's a good thing, or a bad thing."

"You don't know what's in those cars?"

"I don't know for certain if there was *anything* in them."

Lucas thought a moment and then shook his head.

"I can't say they are no problems at the nuke site," Lucas said, putting his things back in his shoulder bag. "We wouldn't be the first to know, we know that. But we would have heard something by now. It would have come down the line if the lake was dirtied by the nuke. No matter how confidential, we would have heard something, Juda. A peep, if nothing else."

Lucas glanced at his friend, who was still surveying the shadowy tables scattered throughout the atrium. But there were only the usual people, office nine-to-fivers and agency workers like themselves. Juda has a more distrusting nature and Lucas knows it.

"And even if one of the reactors melted down, it wouldn't send effects upstream where there is no stream to begin with."

Juda drummed the table and shrugged.

"I told you about the boxcars and you don't care," he told Lucas. "I explain there is secrecy at the nuke site, and you don't care."

"Secrecy is doctrine for our government," Lucas said.

* * *

Months ago, the government embedded moles in the hut city. Gail hired a young family—a father, mother, and two sons, who were on the exodus from Alabama, the site of widespread ruin and death caused by plague-like outbreaks, ultra-religious slaughter, and the total evacuation of police and military—to live among the hut people.

The citoyens themselves were staggering from privations. A disease was spreading—a rampant cough and leaky eyes, the first signs of a germ that would wipe out thousands. It snowed a heavy, foul snow for weeks on end. Animals died. Mothers wept for their children. The healthy young family was thought to bring an infusion of vigor during a time of weakness.

They shaved their heads, the man allowing his facial hair to grow per the custom in the huts. They asked him what he could do—as in, what was his specialty, if any—and he said animals. He had worked on a pig farm since he was a boy. His first pair of shoes had been those rubber boots worn in the troughs and pens. He said he knew cows, goats and horses.

"What about chickens"? they asked.

"Everybody knows about chickens; chickens are easy," the man said. His sons already knew enough to raise a large brood between them. They had done it in Alabama. "Look at the bones," he said, pointing to necklaces they wore. Certain vertebrae from roosters were used, signifying bloodlines, breeds, farms and grangers. This was an exotic detail suggested by Gail. It reminded him of old camps he'd seen in Virginia, with deep-flowing superstitious influences. People who had lived along the James River—people who had died violently, much like the early settlers who'd lived on those soil-rich lands.

Weekly, the man provided Gail with logistical information and updates. Gail wanted to know where the vulnerable sections were, the keeps they shared, the food stores, stoves, ovens, the crude medicines they buried in the mud to keep them preserved. He wanted to make sure they could be wiped out with a single stroke, so as to suppress the stories that seep out of such slaughters—stories that often bloom into uprisings. The Alabama man did not know how Gail planned to wipe them out. He assumed it would involve weapons, a military strike. He told his wife to expect to hear helicopter rotors in the moments before the attack. They kept bags ready (hidden in crawl spaces under their hut), and a plan for narrow escape that they shared with the boys.

Gail promised they would earn refuge in a cool, sunny Northern cove within miles of Canada. The man boasted to his wife that he would fish, she would teach crop sciences (their heritage of the South), and the boys would enter military schools. Gail ensured him this would happen.

As the weeks rolled by, the mole joined the citoyens in deep, dark discussions about their world. Their children were dying in alarming numbers, and healthy ones regularly sneaked off to the capital city, never to return. There was fear that the community would not survive a new pestilence or natural disaster. They were in the crosshairs and they knew it. A new leader—a young, strong, demented man who rarely slept—was forcing them to dig tunnels all around the lake. He was possessed with the idea of returning to caves.

Gail instructed his mole to get involved in the construction of these caves. Gail knew the caves would be impenetrable by soldiers and he instructed his man to take the highest position available, behind the new leader.

The young sons took jobs with the excavation. They joined a crew burrowing into the low, stony hills surrounding the lake. They proved to be good workers. Their father was brought in to meet with the leader, who insisted on the title "Sergeant."

The sergeant sat the mole down and listened to the story of how the family had lived in Alabama, struggling to survive, and then fleeing via a route previously used by 18th century slaves. The sergeant checked the man's arms for military or government tattoos. His loose, oily eyes, as dark as the stones being dug for the caves, roved the mole's torso, legs and shoulders. The sergeant's dirty fingers rubbed the skin that was once tanned and smoothed by bright Alabama sun. The sergeant turned the mole around to face him and searched the man's eyes for something.

"We cannot trust you," the sergeant told him. He was not one of them, and Alabama's horrors included government informants who cost entire settlements their lives.

The mole insisted he could be trusted. Look at his scars.

The sergeant shook his head. He said the man and his family would have to move on once the caves and tunnels were finished. The mole would not be allowed to communicate with the inner circle.

Gail took the news in cold silence. The man asked what he should do. Gail did not answer. Hiding in tall marsh grass on a remote, far end of the lake, the mole whispered into his button, "What are my next steps?"

Gail hung up.

The wife was furious. Were they exposed? Could they even risk sending the boys down into the tunnels and caves again? What would happen now?

It began to rain. Everyone huddled inside their cold rooms and all work stopped. Fires were lit in covered pits, hissing pyres that attracted the sick and dying. The man watched a feeble old woman drop to her knees in the mud beside the main fire, a smoke-billowing cathedral where corpses were being thrown. She wailed and beat her small fists into her face. People turned away. The rain came down harder and the smoke thickened.

"This is worse than Alabama," the wife said.

The man agreed, turned to look at his sleeping sons, just as the first wall of floodwaters came across the lake.

Gail came to the hut city a week later, escorted by soldiers in white fabric suits and lighted masks. The carnage matched the reports. The dead were everywhere, already spoiled by visits from buzzards. They were sprayed with a napalm-like chemical, choking the woods with black exhaust.

Gail took off his gloves so his skin could feel the air. He held them up in front of his mask.

"Your man is over there." One of the soldiers pointed to a body near the entrance to a small, crude tunnel. The mole's mouth was stretched wide open, as if something enormous had tried to get out. The teeth were bent forward and the tongue was gone. Gail bent over and looked at the eyes, which had gone gray, mirroring the sky. There was a single bullet hole in the neck and another in the back of the head.

Gail stood up and put his gloves back on.

"He watched them die," Gail mused to a nearby soldier.

"Yes sir."

"His family," Gail clarified. "Look at his eyes. See what he is seeing? That's him watching his wife and sons die. They … these animals, they murdered his family right in front of him. See his eyes, see where they're looking?" Gail took a couple of short steps, stood on a bed of leaves and pine needles trampled flat into the muck. "Right here. This is where they were. Probably looking right at him. Animals, total animals."

The soldier looked away as thunder rolled in the west.

"Where are the rest of them?" Gail asked the soldier.

"No idea, sir. They could be mixed in with …" He pointed to the bonfire of corpses down the hill. Soldiers were throwing more torches onto the heap.

"Sir, was he military?"

"No. He wasn't government, either. He was nothing. He was caught in-between these animals and us."

The soldier waved down at his buddies in white suits. Some had already started back towards the trucks.

"You want us to get him out, sir?"

Gail shook his head.

"Just throw him on the pile with the others. Burn him up, soldier." He started to walk off and stopped. "Just close his eyes first. I don't want those eyes of his watching me go to the truck. The last thing I need is to think that this piece of filth was watching me leave."

Gail communicated to leadership on his button and reported the scene: no survivors. He looked out of a slash in an otherwise blacked-out window and watched the pines blur by. Suddenly, human forms whipped past. He ordered the convoy to stop and he climbed out, along with a few hand-picked soldiers.

Two soggy, young boys were being dragged along by a woman who bled from her nose. She was shivering so much she couldn't talk.

Gail realized that his mole had not seen them die. He had seen something else, perhaps a pall of gas seeping through the woods, or a flood tide of death. These three had made it out, a miracle. The boys were breathing heavily, talking loudly to their mother.

"Sir?" a soldier said.

Gail thought about it only for a moment. For just a split second he considered showing compassion.

"Shoot them, Soldier, right where they stand."

They crumpled like the wings of a dying bird, the sons collapsing atop their mother. Black blood rolled out of the smaller one's mouth.

* * *

The night the professor leaves, Lucas and Orel go to the movies. There is a movie theater not far from the house. It only shows films on the weekend, and these are always old retreads. They are hoping to catch a comedy because they want to break the sullen mood that the philosopher's exit has caused. Plows have desecrated the sidewalks with mounds of filthy snow and ice, where children have peed, cutting marks into the frozen piles with their urine. There are fires in backyards, in barbecue pits and barrels where impromptu cooks are roasting meats, or where drunken citoyens stagger about, roaring for something violent to happen.

"When do you hear about your exam?" Lucas asks as they wait for a crossing light.

"Two weeks," Orel replies. He crosses first, wondering why they stopped in the first place. The nearest bus is pretty far off, and they can barely hear its knocking motor. One car slowly rolls past as they stand and wait, its driver watching them suspiciously. There are only a few cars out, with nervous drivers glancing and scanning the intersections. Carjacking is not prosecuted anymore, since the government is trying to coerce everyone to ride trains and buses. People are easily tracked on public transportation.

They sit in the front because Orel's mother, Sila, always enjoyed being close to the screen. She said there was charm, a magic, in being so close, that it reminded her of things from growing up that would always give her a warm fuzzy feeling. Lucas said he didn't like being right up under some actor's nose, and she would laugh, covering her mouth with her hand like she did.

It's not a new movie, but it doesn't date back to the old Hollywood studio days. It's from somewhere in between the millennium heyday and the current skeletal cinema culture. Lucas thinks it came out after he married Sila.

"I remember him," Lucas smiles when a young actor with a fiendish glint to his eyes comes onscreen and unleashes a blistering amount of dialogue, also bringing a smile to Orel's face.

"He's hysterical," Orel whispers.

On the way out, they squeeze through the incoming audience, a larger and rowdier group, which is always the case for later shows. People are so drunk for the midnight shows that Lucas thinks a pickpocket could make a good living. The drunks have been known to sleep all night in the seats and then stream out onto the sidewalk in the bright morning sun like zombies.

There is a fight in the lobby and they press against the far wall to go out the door. One frantic kid is against a horde of thuggish young citoyens. Nobody wants to do anything about it, even when the one kid's teeth break and he's shouting through a river of black blood at his attackers.

"So it wasn't always like this?" Orel asks as they take a brisk route home, the bouncy post-movie mood now crushed a bit. Lucas lets out a long sigh and kicks some snow into the gutter.

"For a while, there was just a lot of anxiety," he explains. "Things were just kind of nervous, real skittish. But you don't have that nervousness, that anxiety, anymore. We're resolved now. There was actually more fear in the years before, because everybody had this bottled-up tension that things might turn awful."

A wave of pessimism washed through, some years ago, that drowned the violence that had taken Sila's life. The world has rolled along in a gray, numb state ever since—too drained to lash out at itself. But with the recent souring of the elements, Lucas fears the mood could spin into chaos again, if a building fright—that things can actually worsen—takes hold.

"Does that make sense?" Lucas asks.

"In a sick way," Orel says, "yes."

There is a girl in the street up ahead, down the hill from their house, wearing some type of gown or cape that is illuminated from a light behind her. She floats, her arms out, and sings. They stop and watch. It is hard to tell her approximate age, other than to say she is not old, because her movement is too fluid and effortless. The garment catches the wind and light, trailing her movements like a ghostly companion. Her graceful limbs extend into the night sky, as she twirls and leaps on her pretend stage.

"I don't know what to say about that," Lucas offers at last, as Orel stands transfixed by the performance, wishing he had his camera to capture her strong lines and flowing hair. A crowd slowly gathers and the girl appears to start her routine all over again, from a first position in ballet, palms upward in front of her hips.

* * *

The elite in the government hive have only one true goal: protect those who can afford protection, the Hidden. The hive eliminates the people and places it can no longer protect. It is akin to cutting off a foot caught in a steel trap, an act that must be done without regret, without self-awareness. The shadowy relationship between the Hidden and the government has never been brought into a defining light. Previous generations had explored the tunnels of bribery, symbiotic laws that protected the strong and politically emaciated the weak. But in fifty years, the relationship went from corrupt to criminal. The power between them pulses back and forth, like blood in a sac. Without one, there isn't the other. And for both to survive, they need stone-hearted operatives such as Gail.

Gail has no regrets about the choices he made while navigating his way through the ranks. He has told varying stories, often in threatening scenarios (he never bluffs), as his mood dictates. He knows it began in earnest after a trip to China, when the nation took its nosedive, its spiral into deep corruption, economic madness, and the surrender of hope to save the dying watersheds throughout the country.

He remembers a conversation in D.C. with a thin, well-dressed military type, a man who warned that only a section of the population would make it through the next thirty years. The numbers would dwindle drastically, and fears would escalate, unless the government took steps to veil this approaching misery.

"Think of it as a crummy magic trick," the skinny colonel or whatever said. "There's a hankie, a pause, then a dove, right? Only here, with our trick, the dove is a pile of bones."

Gail visualized medieval paintings of the plague. Crowds of weary, helpless citoyens reeling from years of malignant food and water, left to either die of starvation or be crushed under the treads of merciless tanks.

"Does any of this sound immoral to you?" the colonel asked. It was summer, but not hot, with thickening clouds even then.

"Not especially," Gail said. "It sounds to me like a necessary progression, a continuous track of weeding-out."

"Precisely."

There were great rewards for being complicit with the government, not disappearing being a favorite with all the players.

"Do you think I'm evil?" the colonel asked.

Gail sized up this gentleman. He was an attenuated officer, on the sallow side, but still a trace of former athleticism from years of military training.

"Not particularly. Not in the slightest, I should say."

"Oh, but you should say I am some evil, even if it's just a sliver. We are not in denial amongst ourselves."

Then he remembers arriving to North Carolina, the trains running smoothly then, plenty of arrivals and departures, routes that nearly went cross-country. Gail had a vague smile on his face, almost like a groom arriving to the rehearsal of a loveless but financially rewarding marriage.

He saw the towering glass and metal buildings of the Hidden. They even showed him a model, complete with a grinning, elderly man who enjoyed living in his immaculate dungeon. The place smelled of flowers. What kind, Gail didn't know. He saw that the old man's hands were flaky and trembling, like his own grandfather's, a man who had been executed for treason during the first wave of violence and annihilation.

"Can we trust you?" they asked Gail, their eyes flinty, their faces morbid with their own sacrifices and disavowals. He always told them yes.

The old man in the model touched Gail's hand as Gail was leaving.

"We don't have a choice," the old man smiled thinly. "It is okay for us to do as we see fit. Compassion is a loser's game."

Even the man's breath smelled of flowers. His teeth were white as snow. And although his hands were shaking, his gaze was confident, firm. Gail's grandfather had worn this face, until the last days when he became a rattled, cowardly, stammering husk of defeat. This man in front of Gail had made some hard decisions, all on the right side.

Gail took his hand, shook it, and lifted his chin proudly.

"I am among friends," Gail smiled.

* * *

Goons are in the professor's house, ransacking and looting with all the lights on, making a hellish racket. There isn't much left in there, since what the philosopher didn't transfer to his secure Hidden loft, the movers threw into the back of a spare pickup. Still, thieves will unscrew light bulbs and detach brass and copper fixtures, because you can sell anything at the flea markets, no matter if it's stolen.

There have been houses with their entire HVAC systems dismantled, boxed up and delivered somewhere else, where the savvy thieves will reassemble it and hit the switch, sending cool or warm air rushing through the ductwork, good as gold.

Orel realizes the ballerina in the street is nothing more than a diversion, sent to distract the few responsible or aware people who might be looking out their windows toward the old neighbor's place. Someone is definitely shining a bright spot on her, too luminous and direct for it to be random. This epiphany shatters that wonderful moment of beauty that replayed in a loop in Orel's mind.

"It could just be someone's strange idea of theater," Lucas yawns as they bang around the cabinets for some sort of bedtime snack. "I don't think it would be anyone from around here, but …"

His father stops talking and gives that look, that fatherly incredulity which still appears from time to time: even the eyebrow rises up.

"You have no way of knowing who it is," Lucas says, looking out the kitchen window to the neighboring house, where someone has just smashed one of the massive plate-glass windows in the front. "And neither do I. We probably don't want to know."

Orel finds bread, and the last of their small supply of cinnamon and brown sugar, and says he will make a sweet toast with it. Lucas nods and says he will brew some of that Brazilian coffee. Why save it forever? Don't the beans lose their flavor over time?

He stops at the window and watches what is going on over at the professor's. The curtains are billowing out of a pair of upstairs windows, like prayer flags. There was a time when he thought he could travel to Asia, visit some of the fabled ancient waterfalls, fall in love with whomever he was with— and if he was alone, fall in love with a stranger, or no one at all. There was a little bit of the world left once, but now it is this. Burglary and ballet, arm in arm, as the era of humanity closes through a series of hideous rooms, each one worse than the last.

*   *   *

As the rivers and lakes grow darker and thicker with ruin, as the coastal aquifers turn dry and yield only limestone dust, the higher camps are increasingly paranoid. The directives that typically sputter down are now raining onto Gail's desk. He knows they are watching him. He grasps that they are discussing his grandfather, wondering if he, could surrender to conscience like the old man.

Gail flexes his hands and sits in the atrium, watching workers go to and from elevators, their faces grim. On some, it's like he sees a symbol floating above their heads, the symbol for death. He knows who is marked, and who is not. His heart kicks in his chest as he struggles to evade memories of his disgraced grandfather, a traitor who almost brought the entire family to extinction.

The man went by the name Rubal, a sort of Hindu name that the family pronounced like the Russian currency. He wore a white beard that he let grow thick and wild, from ear to ear and down his neck. He had billowy hair, also white. For much of Gail's childhood he was a mystery, a whisper, a fragment of a dream, until the soldiers appeared.

On a clear blue, cold January day along the shores of the Potomac River in Virginia, on a farm with rolling white fences and fires on the hearths, came a knot of men with service revolvers. They wore berets and black ties, the strangest uniforms Gail had ever seen.

They didn't read Rubal his rights as they took him outside. They restrained him with zip ties. Gail looked at his grandfather's face, suddenly slack as if he had aged greatly on the spot; his eyes were moist as they wrapped a black cloth around his head. Then the old man's lips moved a little.

"I have been sick," he said, softly as though they were caretakers.

One of the men pulled another cloth from his coat and tested it for length to go around Rubal's mouth.

"Not *sick* sick," the grandfather hurried out. "Just my stomach. This morning after breakfast. Nerves, most likely."

They wrapped the cloth around his mouth, stopped him to tie a knot at the back of his head. The white hair fluttered for a moment in the cold breeze. A pair of seagulls flew over, heading upriver. The old man cocked his chin as if he could hear their wings. Then he bowed his head and they led him off.

A few days later it snowed. The family had been silent since the arrest. They shuffled about the rooms, eyes lowered, afraid to speak since the whole place might have still been bugged.

The dogs were inside by the fires, the snow too deep for them outside. And then late one afternoon, as the sky bulged with a somber gray cast, a large truck approached. Men got out. Muscular men with radios on rods attached to their metal helmets. They scowled and walked right in. They carried in large wood lockers and began filling them with his family's belongings, roughly, as Gail remembers. He could hear fragile things break.

Gail stood by the fire in the den and watched the dogs as they watched lockers come swiftly in, then lumber out. The big dog, an old one, yawned so that its chipped yellow teeth showed prominently.

Then all of a sudden they were leaving. It had taken maybe half an hour. One of the last men stopped and spoke quietly with Gail's father and mother. The man kept his eyes on the father as he spoke. He had what looked like snot leaking into his red mustache. This was the way police spoke to criminals, Gail thought. At one point the policeman raised his gloved finger and shoved it into the mother's face. She began to cry. Just quiet tears down her cheeks, no sobbing.

As this last man turned on his boot heel to go, Gail called out to him. The dogs looked over at the boy. The man glared at him and waited. Gail pointed:

"Up there, on the mantle, in that ivory box … there is something really valuable. I have seen them all hold it in secret, whispering so that I couldn't hear them."

The man went over, reached up and carefully removed the lid. Then he took the box down and removed its contents: a rolled parchment scroll, tied with a faded red ribbon.

Gail remembers that a warmth flooded his body, the kind which blushes the cheeks. The man (a captain?) cut his eyes over to the boy. The boy's eyes were as bright as sunlit water.

To this very day, they trace Gail's documentable strain of misanthropy. His file clearly states that the arrest of his grandfather was the turning point. But the first active application of his "patriotism" (they described it, informally, as *a blind allegiance to governing power that borders upon fascism, with sadistic tendencies*) happened during a visit inside a government prison.

Rubal's facility was in the North Carolina mountains, atop a blunt peak in a thick evergreen forest. A cold creek slithered freely over the stones nearby, a stark contrast to the inmates who came along, shackled in chains and leg irons.

At the time, Gail was in a military boarding school, the last of its kind between D.C. and Atlanta. He was a couple of months past his thirteenth birthday. He wore his dress grays, the most immaculate, crisp uniform in his closet.

Gail rode with his parents on a dismal morning just before Christmas. The mountain grades were icy, the air thick with mists, and the stone cliffs appeared to sweat freezing ooze. He hated his parents by this point. He was outraged that they still owned legal control of his life. In a year he would join a Science Cadets program that would wrench him free of them.

On this day, he slouched in the back of their musty car and fogged his window with breath, drawing tombstones upon which he etched their names and dates of death, both December 25th.

A solitary soldier manned the entry gate. He never looked up as they carded in, scanned their barcodes, and slowly rolled down a winding path toward the tiny visitor parking lot. His mother sighed and checked her face in a mirror.

She is ugly, her son thought and said often. She had been in and out of mental asylums since her father-in-law's arrest. She was just weeks away from her own real death, a dramatic suicide in the kitchen of the dank apartment in Richmond they had rented ever since Rubal's farm was taken. She hanged herself from the rusty candelabra, eventually pulling the wires loose so that the whole building (a two-story brick in a ghetto) burned down.

The father sat rigid at the wheel. He had given up the estate to keep the remaining family intact and reasonably safe. The young daughter's removal (virtually all those who disappear are killed) devastated him. He begged Gail's way into military school. He would wander off into oblivion after his wife's suicide, letting the government take over with his son.

On this day, they were treated roughly by the guards who checked them into the visitor area. These were big, heavy men, long-term veterans of the prison who spoke with thick Southern accents. One of the larger guards, a yellow-haired man with a series of faded crude runes tattooed on his face, pushed the father against the wall with a finger to his chest. The father let the guard bring his meaty nose right into his face and growl insults.

Then they sat in an airless, windowless room and waited. A tiny camera in the far corner of the ceiling watched them hang their heads in shame as they prepared for Rubal to be dragged in. And when the old man entered, he was unrecognizable. They had shaved his head and removed the sage white beard. He looked beaten and gaunt. His teeth were ruined and there was a large copper earring dangling on the left side of his head.

"Oh dear," the mother whispered.

The father wrung his hands and as if he didn't know what to do.

"My misfortune is that they haven't killed me yet," Rubal wheezed, as a chair was dragged to the table for him.

The tattooed guard growled and cursed some more. He shoved the old man down into the metal chair.

Gail smelled the old man. He used to carry the scent of horses and linen, but now reeked like a citoyen. A pale pink chemise covered all but his bony, bruised arms. It hadn't been washed in weeks and there were lice crawling all over the stained cloth.

"Talk to him!" the guard ordered. "He's only got ten minutes."

Gail's mother began to weep. A deep, soft, quiet event that brought her hands to her face, as her head bowed toward the table. The father tried to smile. His lips moved, then his tongue appeared, pink as a baby's nose. A few indecipherable words trailed out.

"She's dead, isn't she?" the old man said, his eyes moving cautiously around the room, taking in the ugly cinderblock walls, the greasy green paint smeared on them.

The mother sobbed. The father gave a slight nod. They had buried Rubal's wife just the week before. A heart attack.

"Poor thing," Rubal said.

"And our Gracie," the mother cried out. She shook her fists and glared at the tattooed guard who stood with his thick, hairy arms folded. "Murderers!"

Rubal shushed her, gently as a priest.

"It doesn't do any good," he said quietly. Then he looked at Gail, whose eyes were fixed, without emotion, on his disgraced grandfather. The youth stiffened indignantly.

"They have you, don't they, boy?" said Rubal. "In their cold grasp, you have become the defiant, loyal-to-the-enemy one. Am I right?"

Gail licked his lips and leaned slightly forward.

"I wish I could execute you myself," he said.

4.

Orel gets a rush when he rides the train. He has been riding these trains all his life, and has been traveling solo a great deal since his mother's death. Over the past year, as he's really gotten into the groove of homeschooling, he has been exploring the depths of the city, its blighted fringes, and the ghostly hamlets where boarded houses and stores are home to some of the worst citoyens.

He has been riding the train all day, reading from a book of poems. He watches the faces on the train, the tired clerks and soldiers who sink into their seats to doze a bit, the paranoid laborers who seem to be gazing through the windows (but are actually scanning the reflections of others on the train), and the housewives who Orel likes to think are praying into their folded hands, appealing to providence for safe journeys in and out of the city.

The best days are when someone decides to spike the volume of the music pumped into the cars. It is usually a muted undercurrent, this industrial electronica from a hundred years before. Usually he can't even hear it if someone is snoring or talking on their button. But when the volume surges, it is fantastic, like being in a film.

Today it has been loud for a couple of stops when Orel is nearly to his station, the Green Eno Nine. The morning fog has all burned off and snow has melted from all the streets and sidewalks. He thinks he has seen the yellow blur of jonquils or daffodils streaming along the tracks not far back. A lady up front in the car said as much, tapping happily at the glass as she pointed this out to nobody in particular.

This will be Orel's last spring here and he worries how his father will do, alone and always thinking of water. He sees how Lucas hunches over, writing at his desk downstairs, in a cramped room that is always dark and fragrant—fragrant with the scent of mild anxiety, as he describes it in his journal. Lucas is trying to keep some things from the past alive, documenting life as he can.

"My great-great-grandfather was a poet," Lucas has proudly told him. "He was a professor at Black Mount College, before the world was in ruins and there were better joys to express, other than 'I didn't die today.'"

Orel crams one of his old great-great-grandfather's leather-bound poems into his back pocket, zips his coat, wraps the leather scarf around his face, and tramps off the train with a few others. He almost has butterflies in his stomach, this happy feeling of being free and about to become even freer. He will miss his father, but maybe Lucas can come up North to live, since surely there is not as much spoiled groundwater up North as there is here.

And they have some family up there. Old New Yorkers and Bostonians who, Lucas insists, have joined the reclusive Hidden in their giant, skeletal cities. You don't hear from these people until they're dead, and then all you get is a rubber box on your doorstep filled with all sorts of strange things, from titles for god-knows-where-they-are automobiles, to glittery wedding rings that have been passed down through generations.

Orel is trying to track down and communicate with some of the uncles who live in Brooklyn. Pushing through the web of layers that protect the Hidden is difficult, but not impossible. It could just make things easier, knowing he could take refuge with family if he needed to. It would surely give Lucas some relief.

He checks the home email service and there is nothing about his university application. Maybe it will come soon. He takes out some frozen meat and lays it in the sink to thaw for dinner. He taps on the Dolby system, and the strain of a zipper orchestra fills the upstairs rooms. He looks out his bedroom window as he peels off his layers, peering around the façade to the corner of the professor's house and its newly blackened windows.

Across the yard, through a glassless window in the upstairs of the professor's abandoned house, Orel watches a skinny, shirtless man, arguing with a distraught young girl. The man's face is a square; the girl's is a moon. Rage and despair. This grizzled intruder corners her, his muted raging words causing to flinch and hug the wall. She is weeping through shut eyes as she tries to escape his grip. Orel would swear this is the same girl he and his father saw performing in the street that night. It was just a couple nights ago, surely he would know her if he saw her. But while she was radiant then, her beauty was contorted in this scene of violence and desperation.

The man's fierce silver eyes flash out the window at Orel. The intruder has ugly deep-set eyes, broken nose, and a tattoo of a spider on his neck, its web drifting down his shoulder and chest. He shakes his fist at his onlooker, quickly draws the curtain, and the execrable scene ends.

Orel doesn't know what to do. He is frozen. Calmly he pulls his curtains, realizing he should have done this already, and puts on clothes to wear around the house. Numbly he goes into the kitchen, heats the oven, and begins the prep for his meatloaf, which he wants to have ready by six.

* * *

Gail is a dark presence in Lucas's department, a brooding and pithy leader whose steely eyes do most of his talking. There is fear among the engineers and scientists who have been in government long enough to know what Gail does—the disappearances of their colleagues, the inhuman, calculating policies he imposes. They tread lightly in the halls, and cower at their desks, simply trying to remain invisible to him if they can. Today, Gail has called a meeting of the minds at Water Purification and the grapevine says he is about to drop a bombshell.

"I'll believe it when I see it," Lucas tells a pair of biologists in the elevator. They are leaning back against the faux wood walls drinking coffee from special stainless steel canisters. One of them was the guy who first detected bromine was leeching into the water systems. He joked he got a medal for that, but that it was coated in mercury, so he had to throw it away.

"It's going to be about the Harris nuke site," the other biologist says. "There are all kinds of whispers going around."

"I know, I've heard some," Lucas says as he looks at the panel and watches the numbers light up while they climb to Gail's floor. "But it's more of an incident report than an analysis."

"What have you heard?" the medal-winner asks.

Lucas wags his head.

"Probably the same thing you guys have."

"Probably."

"Gail was going out of his mind all last week," the other one cuts in, leaning forward like he is talking to the floor, as they slow down for their stop. "I saw him in the lobby on Thursday, sitting on one of the couches, and I think he was holding a conversation with an invisible man."

"No button?" the medalist says as the doors open.

"He wasn't on a phone. He was talking to thin air."

There is a sea of suits around Gail's door, a lot of faces Lucas has never seen. There are anxious faces, with plastic badges around their necks, sweating through their jackets. This crowd reminded Lucas of what he to see all the time when the directives were flying to evacuate the lower mountains. This was what sent the population sprawling in either direction, way upriver or down. It was all the result of a leak at the nuke in the rural highlands of a place named Sophia. It was a new plant, and there has always been speculation that it was sabotaged. Lucas heard endless revisions from people like Juda. Some people think if you unplugged all the nuke sites the planet would recover.

Lucas doesn't know what the solution is, but he knows they are heading down a path to greater destruction. He does not like Gail, but knows this man does not like to lose. And by the look on his face right now, it seems he has lost in a big way.

"Folks," Gail says as they crowd around his desk, "the end is not nigh, but I am telling you that it has begun its slow creep upon us. The only way I can be certain about this is that there is so much uncertainty from all around. From above, from D.C. All the channels. Uncertainty and disorder is everywhere."

Gail explains that uncertainty equals a worsening of already squalid conditions.

"Improvement is impossible," he says. "Survival is all we have."

The woman next to Lucas starts to fidget. Her stomach might be upset, with all the noises going on inside her. He wonders what it would be like if someone in the room actually soiled themselves. There is a chance it could go unnoticed, all things considered. Then she raises her hand, kind of flashes it over her head before yanking it down.

"Can I make a comment?" she asks, in a distressed, shaky voice.

"No," Gail sighs. He is staring at this black glass globe on his desk, rocking gently in his chair. "There are a few people around here who have been involved in a decision-making process or two. We feel compelled to make the choices that others won't. The impact of these choices … is broad and unpleasant." He rolls his eyes over the room.

Gail takes a pause, strokes his long, buzz-cut head, flexes his jaw muscles, and goes back to staring at his desk globe.

"We are shutting off the water to all outliers," he says. "From here on out, they will have to fend for themselves."

"You know the wells aren't safe anymore," someone in the back says.

Gail speaks slowly, softer this time. "We are shutting off all public water, to all outliers."

"They'll die," someone whispers.

"They will panic for sure," the woman beside Lucas says, bewildered.

Gail reaches out and spins his globe so that it turns slowly enough for him to watch the continents swing round and round.

"I wanted you to hear it from me," Gail tells them. He apologizes that this is not a meeting where questions are answered.

Another person in the back, walks out the door as he says it takes a coward to make such an unconscionable decision. Lucas nods in agreement, but doesn't speak out.

"Folks, that is all," Gail says as he gives the globe another easy spin.

*   *   *

Of all the things in life made obsolete by changes to the world, food is what Lucas misses most. Food is so different now that he cannot properly explain it to Orel how it used to be. Even the places they bought groceries, he can't describe this to a youth who has never seen row after row of cereals, canned fruits, condiments, pasta and sodas. Orel only knows the little markets and the entitlements (he and his father are lucky enough to be included in this program) for government workers.

There are still some restaurants, but the old neon-lit chains are gone. Now it is a scattered arrangement of owner-operated dives, and the occasional place that boasts cuisine from the past. On Thanksgiving they will go get a couple of plates of meatloaf (it at least *seems* like real beef), and it fascinates Orel that there used to be such an option, on any day, to eat out like that. Lucas has to make these reservations well in advance. They can neither afford nor find the pull to go out for Christmas meals. But Christmas isn't what it used to be, so that doesn't matter much.

The markets are another story. There are bartering places, service-for-trade places (these often only deal in sex-only trades), drug-exchange operations, and a few co-ops, with the ID-only markets rounding out the options. This is where Lucas and Orel shop: government-run and subsidized, small but with many locations. Open at all hours. Armed cashiers keep out the citoyens and outliers.

In the past, Lucas shopped when a cashier was still mopping blood off the floor because a bold citoyen had stormed an ID market, seeking fresh vegetables or meat. These clerks and cashiers are surly, dangerous people who are vying for the means to get back into better roles in government offices; they are rewarded for killing.

The citoyens mostly trade and barter, with a portion of their needs being met through theft and chicanery. They ooze out of their dirty dwellings to beg and steal what they cannot swindle within their ghettos.

There are outer parts of the city, where animals are raised including the ugliest creatures—goats, chickens and such—god ever brought into existence. On these crude "farms" you will find the citoyens who reject the authority of the military and government. They want nothing of the world that people such as Gail seek to preserve and protect. They want out just as badly as Gail wants them out. But they need an opportunity, an event that would distract or disperse the military, which holds such a grip on everyone and all things.

Lucas goes out and inspects the water on these farms monthly, and finds it steadily worsening. It's not the pipes—they are PVC and relatively new, from the perspective of the government. Nor is it the household plumbing. The fixtures vary wildly from hovel to hovel, and often from kitchen to bathroom. But Lucas believes it is the supply itself. Someone must have contaminated it; it is the only way to explain the downhill skid they have taken out on the farms.

Of late he deals with a woman, a brown-skin with a cleft palate, who shares a three-room basement crawler with two children and an epileptic male. The man is most likely her brother, because he has been tormented by neighbors for being a homosexual. The woman is thirty or so and complains that the water makes her children sick with diarrhea on a regular basis. Her brother is sick every day, so he lies on a cot in the kitchen where the only window, high up the ceiling, brings in a damp breeze.

The woman has stopped showing Lucas her children. She says they are afraid of him, and fearful of all the government people who are poisoning everybody they know. He asks why they say this.

"Because it's true," the woman says, looking at her poor brother. "And everyone says it now, whether it gets back to the snitches or not. We're not all afraid of you. Some of us could be willing to take a stand."

"Against what?" he asks.

She lifts a cloth from her brother's forehead and sees that he is asleep.

"Murder," she says. "A hundred years of it."

She checks her brother's cheek for fever. There is sorrow in her mannerisms, a compelling air of attachment which strikes Lucas as uncommon among the citoyens, especially here on the outer edges. Her lip is busted and he wonders about it. Then she looks at him with her dark, large eyes.

"I worry about my children," she says. "What kind of life will they have? Will it be a life at all? And what kind of world will be left for them when *you* have finished tormenting us?"

The woman's voice rises as she turns fully toward Lucas. She expects him to dismiss everything she has said. She concentrates hard to express her grief, her lifetime of struggle which she has shared with so many of her neighbors.

"There isn't an inability to love out here," she says, her eyes fixed on his. "There's just so little time and energy for it."

He grows uncomfortable listening to her because he has never heard a citoyen say anything even remotely profound. There is also the guilt that he knows what she says is true.

"Do you have children?" she asks him.

"One. A son."

She looks away. There is a noise out in the street above.

"You should get him out of here," she says. "It would be easy for you, compared to me. All you need is the will to do it."

She is working towards a pragmatic solution for them both: He flees, she stays; let their outcomes be decided by fate. The only flaw in her logic is her ignorance of people like Gail—hunters who hunt their own kind, as well as the enemy.

"You should get him an antibiotic," he tells her, gesturing to her brother. "It would help him pretty quickly. It's called 'Cephalosporin,' the type he needs. I'll write it down for you."

She laughs, but nods, and lets him lay a piece of paper by the filthy sink. On the back he writes out the name of the antibiotic, like a parent writes to his child, the letters comically large. It is a blank controlled document that he uses to track contamination. On the front, his name is at the top, as is Gail's, with an address. He says goodbye to her, puts a vial of her tap water in his coat, and hurries out. He climbs a dark stairwell to reach the street. It is pouring rain and the van he came in is parked farther down, its lights flashing and the driver talking on the radio loudspeaker, issuing a warning to someone to stay clear of the van. The driver, a young man new to Purification, sounds scared, and his voice rises and falls throughout each repeated warning.

Lucas stops as someone hurls a flaming jar at the van. The young assistant screams over the loudspeaker, an almost comical shriek that startles some rooftop pigeons into flight. Lucas sprints toward the van. The Molotov cocktail's flames have been sizzled out by the rain. Soot streaks the windshield until the assistant gets the wipers going.

"Useless animals!" the guy yells as Lucas climbs in. "Can you believe this?" the assistant growls as he inspects his weapon, a handheld automatic, and pops the safety off. "I should spray these rejects."

Lucas points to drive off, just get them the hell out. But the guy has a problematic look on his face. So far, this assistant is like most others Lucas has come across—entitled, boring, more than a little stupid, and openly hostile towards any form of real work. This ultra-violent stance towards the citoyens is new.

"Drive us back," Lucas says. There is no one out on the street now. The rain is coming harder.

The assistant chews his lip. The temper in his eyes changes.

"Are you against me killing them?"

"Yes," Lucas says.

"I figured. And are you against the government?"

"No," Lucas says. "What the hell is wrong with you?"

The guy puts them in gear and they pull off, tires squalling. The wipers beat a steady rhythm. They roll through an intersection–that is flanked by crippled traffic signals. The utility wires are festooned with makeshift flags, tatters of trash, and ropes the citoyen children use to climb up to their lookout points atop dead transformers.

The skyrises appear, as the van blows through a citoyen-filled underpass. The top of the city is shrouded in mist, and the streets are skimmed with muddy runoff. Lucas gazes along the dashboard until he sees the assistant's button glowing in its mount. Just barely, without turning his head any more, he can see the details of the last call in: an encrypted number attached to Gail.

* * *

Every day for lunch, Gail eats at a nook between government warehouses, a place with dirty windows, tattered awnings, and a broken marquee that has only a few hissing red bulbs. This used to be a place where people sat and laughed. You could get plates of roast beef with gravy, hand-mashed potatoes, even pie.

Gail rolls his eyes along the wet pavement, the alley where a group of sour-smelling citoyens often hunch over a makeshift fire in a barrel. He pats the knife—a dagger they gave him in D.C. "to open serious and secret mail, ha-ha"—in his coat and stops just before the door, when he sees one of them come out of the alley.

The citoyen is thin, bearded, and filthy with those milky eyes of someone who has not eaten protein for an eternity. The man picks his nose and stares sullenly. Gail turns so they face each other.

"I see you a lot," the citoyen says, his teeth badly rotted.

Gail nods. He knows he is taller, stronger, and has hate on his side. The citoyen is gimpy, and as he talks the dirty face reveals a disfigurement Gail knows is caused by venereal disease.

"You must have good work," the derelict continues. "It takes a real job to be able to come out for lunch every day."

"This place is a dump," Gail responds, holding his ground as the man edges closer.

"Even so."

Gail smells the sour flesh and the filthy clothes, the ugly breath the citoyen pulls out of his lungs. He knows this man, who is maybe thirty, has not eaten well in years. Perhaps he has forgotten what a good meal tastes like, what food that's not laced with pollution and waste does on the tongue.

"You're lucky," the citoyen sneers. He glances at the windows of the little restaurant, wipes his long nose and blinks at the murky light inside, the shadows of people eating and carrying trays of food.

"Not lucky," Gail corrects, smiling thinly as one hand slips into his coat. "Just very determined."

The citoyen taps his bony finger on the glass and shows his bad teeth again. He looks Gail up and down.

"Why do you come here every day if it's such a dump?"

Gail stays relaxed as he opens the blade in his pocket and lifts it out, slowly, like it is hot to the touch. He leans the blade to the left, then to the right, akin to wagging a sharp finger disapprovingly.

"Why do I? Probably the same reason you huddle there in that alley, waiting for something to happen," he says, pointing the knife past the citoyen. "We get used to what we do, and after a while it doesn't even occur to us that we could do anything different. Why would we want to? So why should I *not* come here? Where do you suggest I go?"

It starts to drizzle, and the citoyen scans the empty street, probably looking for the rest of his group. It appears he cannot see well and he steadily wipes his eyes. He asks what Gail knew he would ask. Gail knows the others have slipped off to go begging for food or money, or they've strayed into slums for drinking, fighting and bleeding out. They surely saw his suit, his shoes and coat, his ring, the pin on his lapel. But this one did not.

Gail watches the milky eyes turn his way. The sneer has vanished. What remains is a lonely face smeared with weeks of grime. Gail puts his knife away and tells him to wait right here by the window, where he stands now, and he will come back and bring food and money.

"Stay where I can see you," Gail says.

In the restaurant he finds his little table near the back and sits, pulls out his button and makes a call while he orders. The waiter looks out the window before moving to Gail's table.

"Is he with you?" the waiter asks.

"No," Gail says. "But he will be gone in a minute." There is silence at the tables, with most of the patrons staring into their food. They have grown mute since Gail came in. A few are hurrying to leave, noisily finishing. A cook in the kitchen curses and breaks a dish on the floor.

Through the dirty window, Gail watches as four soldiers approach the citoyen. They grab him by the head and shoulders and force him to the sidewalk. They beat him with batons.

"Here is your coffee, sir," the waiter says.

"Thank you," Gail smiles.

A young woman hurries to the door, a government worker who knows Gail by sight. She is throwing her coat on, waiting for the man with her to pay at the counter behind Gail. She looks away when Gail's eyes find her. Gail is blowing into his mug when the man passes, a big man with a cheap coat, probably from the legal division. The man suddenly turns and glares at Gail.

"Isn't it bad enough," he snarls, "that they … they live like they do, without even so much as a glimmer, a little sliver of hope to ever be better? That's not enough for you?"

"It isn't," Gail says. "That is not enough, not for me."

He eats slowly, drinks four cups of coffee. Only a few dour faces remain: university people, bored government workers, a nervous elderly couple at the very back, in shadows, who whisper in bursts. He figures they are candidates for Hidden in a nearby skyrise, awaiting word on their status. The woman raps her rings on the old wood table and sighs while the man, her husband, goes on and on, quietly, urgently.

As he leaves, Gail inspects the sidewalk by the door. Blood is thickening in splatters around a brown tooth nearby. He is careful not to get his shoes in it as he propels his umbrella into the soft rain. Heading back to his office, he taps out a message on his button, turns a block early and finds the rear of the legal division building. There are two citoyen boys leaned against a Dumpster, smoking the butts they've found inside it. They wear white wristbands to signify that their parents are in prison camps. These are the worst of the worst. Gail touches his knife again.

"Faggot!" one of the boys yells as Gail passes, ten yards away from them, in the center of a service road between buildings. A bank of groaning HVAC boxes roar to life, hissing steam, as Gail folds up his umbrella and waits at the bottom step for a door to open. He turns briefly again to the boys who, being the hoodlums they are, have started to urinate on a dead dog beside the dumpster.

The door opens and out comes the lawyer who chided him at lunch, just a few minutes before. The lawyer is dismayed, escorted by soldiers who wear metal helmets and hard scowls. His eyes bulge with fear and his lips move wordlessly until he sees Gail; then he starts kicking at the handrails.

Gail mounts three steps, looks into the lawyer's eyes, and sees what he has seen so often in recent years: indignation towards the fall. He takes out his knife and punctures the lawyer's white dress shirt until it is awash in red. The lawyer cries out, forcing the soldiers to punch his mouth until he stops. Then Gail cuts his throat and signals that he is to be left there to die.

Gail goes back down the steps, wiping his knife, and keeps his eyes on the boys as he goes past. They smoke silently now, the crackle of their dirty butts the only sound. Gail stops.

"I *am* lucky," he says. "I try to hide it, but it shows anyway. Can't you see it?"

The taller boy, his head wrapped in rags, the one who called Gail a faggot, shrugs and looks away to the slab where the lawyer's blood still glistens. They can smell it.

"Maybe not," Gail sighs. "Maybe you have to be like me to know what I am."

* * *

Capturing the ideal black-and-white photograph is what Orel strives to do. The underground photojournalism movement exploded when he was a kid, following the demolition of mainstream newspapers and magazines. Traditional media was taken down by hordes of angry hackers who felt they had been lied to for way too long. In its wake came a renegade army of people who built protocols for their transmissions.

First and foremost, the truth must be told. Inspiration is encouraged. And beauty, what there is left of it, must play its part.

Orel delivers sporadic submissions, but has never really given anything that wasn't solely of local interest. After what he saw in his neighbor's window, the old hoary intruder terrorizing the ballerina, he thinks he may have something that could spread on this site.

He was holding his camera and took two shots out his window, without raising it to look at the viewfinder, before he closed his curtain. It was a reflex. He takes shots of everything. It was on the corner of his dresser and he picked it up without thinking and squeezed twice before it was over with. While he is busy testing his images, his father stays outside to do something in the yard.

"Orel!" his father shouts from downstairs. "Come help me outside!"

He calls back. He saves the file and then sends it, with text that explains what little he knows specifically of this scene but so well of a broader, far-reaching problem: Humanity is in steep decline. Tomorrow's perils, while unknown today, will be hellish.

He bounds down the back stairs and into the yard. Lucas is stooped over something at the property line, where massive iron trellises once held thickets of roses and such. In a dry stone fountain there, someone has tossed the corpse of the ballerina. She is naked and blue, her hands bound by an electrical cord. Her eyes stare dreamily at their shoes.

Orel has too much adrenaline rushing through him to stop and think creatively. Going on instinct, he raises the viewfinder of his camera and takes a single image of the girl. It is a crisp image and the negative space is balanced perfectly in the center around the girl. A few stray leaves are played across her body providing contrast from her deep color to her bloodless skin. She is defiled, yet still beautiful, in the way a dead bird lies enchanted in the mud, its wings contorted, while a strange, aching promise of flight lingers.

"I wonder what happened," Lucas says, rubbing his chin like you do when an engine won't start but you still have a feeling that you can get it going. He has seen a lot of carnage and waste over the years, and he doesn't realize this is their street dancer.

"Who would just leave her here like this?" he asks, turning to Orel. There isn't much of a reason to call the police, because they will not come, not from all the way in the city. So they call the street department and ask if they can swing by and pick up a corpse today while they are out pushing the last of the snow and ice from the curbs. It's the least they can do, says the street department woman on the other end.

So they sit on the front terrace with some of their Brazilian coffee and wait for a truck to come around to retrieve the girl. The sun is trying to ply its way through the midday clouds, and Lucas says they will have to go the market later, once the street workers have come around and gotten the body. The freezer is almost empty and the cabinets are not far behind.

"We're not going to be able to live here any longer, Dad," Orel says, watching the horizon where birds used to drive their flocks in spring, but now who can say where they are?

"I know," Lucas says. "We'll stock up for a move at the market today. First thing in the morning, we head out."

Brutal murders such as this one are increasingly more common. But Lucas knows that when they arrive at your doorstep, it is best to get moving.

5.

Tall black trees spill over the hills as Lucas drives an unheated four-door sedan toward the Haw River, their belongings packed like stones in the backseat and trunk. There are chunks missing from the rural roads that force Lucas to keep his speed down, which allows Orel to hang out his window snapping pictures—that leather scarf wound tightly around his face to keep it from freezing.

They will zoom for a stretch, winding around back roads flanked by twisted hawthorn trees and glazed quartzite the size of tents, as Orel waves vaguely at children standing in fortified yards, rifles clutched to their sides.

"Will they shoot us?" he asks.

"They want us to think they will," Lucas answers. "We're supposed to believe it, and I think it's best if we seem to."

There is a bridge over a foamy creek at one point, connecting with a waterfowl impoundment nearby, which stinks so much it burns their nostrils. Lucas swipes at the vent levers but air seeps in anyway, until they are past it in a blur and the car slams through a series of jarring potholes.

"Gadsen's old Buick," he tells his son, "can't take many more of those."

The tales of roadblocks prove false and they reach their destination without any trouble whatsoever, despite shoddy roads. This is a locale, Lucas has heard, that may have untainted groundwater, as well as a safe community of peaceniks. These are folk who still farm, even tend livestock, and protect their land without violence, using the fables of haunted woods and churches and graveyards to keep hooligans away.

"I've never seen anything like this before," Orel says, as they come to rest at the foot of a gravel entrance to a place concealed by leafless willow oak. They can hear the hiss of a stream rushing through giant wet stones, smell the smoke of fires, and see how the low-flung clouds force dark shadows throughout the river valley. "I can see how it's easy to make people believe it has ghosts."

Lucas smiles. "These old mill towns scare the bejesus out of citoyens, who aren't religious, or spiritual, or deep thinkers in any way. The religious took to the high hills and mountains, dropping anchor in the Blue Ridge when the nuke went awry in Sophia." He has yet to understand why people in the city fear these docile hamlets. Unless it is just because of ghost stories.

"Spooky is the term," he says, still smiling, to his son. "It's an outdated conceit. You wouldn't understand, and I'm not sure I do, either. But it has something to do with our brains, when our brains used to be disquieted by notions of the afterlife."

"That's weird."

"Yeah. There is so much now that we deal with, where life is concerned, just living our lives, that it's kind of hard to wrap your head around getting all worked up over evil spirits."

Orel nods and looks out his window, up into the gnarled shrubs on his side of the road. There is a car battery caked in mud with jumper cables attaching it to a calf-high iron rod in the ground. There is also what looks like an old Spanish sword stabbed into a bed of pink wildflowers.

"I do feel like we're being watched," Orel says.

"But that's every day of our lives."

"I can still feel it though."

"You're right. It doesn't go away."

"What are we going to do now?" Orel asks.

"I don't know. I hadn't figured out anything besides just getting us here."

"I understand."

Lucas wipes his face with a bandana. The air is so damp here. Must be the streams and the river, he thinks.

"They weren't happy with me at work," he says after a few minutes, once it is clear nothing is going to happen any time soon. "Gail, my boss, said it is the most crucial time at Water Purification, and that I'm a coward for bailing out right now."

"You've always said Gail had trouble negotiating between his own interests and that of the common good. Why would his opinion matter to you now?"

"He seemed to be making a turn. I thought maybe he was starting to get it."

"We had to get out, Dad."

"I know."

"After that guy hurting that girl …"

"You can die trying to catch your train."

"We had to leave while we could."

Lucas turns to his son, who has his glass out and is swiping through a sea of photographs, looking for his picture, the one of the ballerina. But it must have been moved or deleted because he can't find it anywhere. Lucas wonders what will become of him, if there is even any reason for him to go off to college, other than to hide away in the last refuge for the young: the North. Economists are saying the global markets should have collapsed already and sent every nation back into medieval scales. And the philosophers, like the professor, have surrendered. Politicians who hold seats voluntarily are scarce. Every week feels like the last week. Lucas wonders how a boy like Orel has hope.

Orel looks up and squints.

"What?"

Lucas shakes his head. The car, Gadsen's Buick, shudders against a gust of gray wind. They take a small meal in silence, bread and hummus. They drain a canister of coffee (the end of their Brazilian) and shake off some of the cold that is now gripping their spot. They are a hundred yards from the stream (all that remains of the Haw River here) and a crumbling concrete span that bridges this deserted town from a hillside of huts, shacks and geodesics.

They pass a monocular back and forth, but all the hillside windows are blacked out. Lucas figures this is where the people are. The only information he has to go on is that if you sit and wait, somebody will eventually come out and talk with you. But he is starting to think Juda didn't know what he was talking about. The idea that somebody is going to stroll down that hill …

Somebody bangs on the rear windshield, hard.

"Christ!"

Then somebody yanks Orel's door open, forcing it open since the door is locked. And a large dirty hand comes in and snatches the boy out by his coat.

"Hey! Hey!" Lucas is outside the Buick yelling, stunned by how many people are out here. How did six people sneak up on them?

A stocky redhead woman yanks a pipe from inside her sheepherder coat and waves it at him. There are several long-legged men in coveralls, their ponytails tied with colorful ribbons, shouldering axes and sledgehammers, who give Lucas and Orel menacing looks.

"The bridge is out," the woman growls, "so you can't cross. And what I want to know is, since you can see that as good as any of us, why are you just sitting here in your crappy LeSabre?"

One of the men, who must be nearly seven feet tall, gently takes Orel's tablet away and starts looking over screens.

"We came here to stay," Lucas says dully, inadvertently making fists and taking a wide stance.

"Nobody stays here," the man who took Orel's computer says.

The woman tosses her metal pipe from one hand to the other.

"Wait, Gerard," she says with a grin, "this guy looks like he doesn't know what he has walked into …"

"Or out of," Gerard cuts in.

Lucas shows them his palms and wags his head like a thief caught red-handed. It's difficult to read the mood. Are they pissed off or not?

"I'm a bioengineer," he says. "And we can't stay in the city any longer. It's not safe. My son is an artist. He is going away in the fall, to school. I can stay here and help."

"With what?"

"Water. I fix water."

Several of them laugh.

"Not lately you haven't," Gerard sneers.

"Seriously," the woman chuckles. "You can't park here, Mr. Bioengineer."

They are laughing amongst themselves and turning to walk back into the tiny deserted town.

"He cleaned the salmon fry ponds in '58," Orel says. "The ones that still produce Coho. We think we could build an operational salmon farm here."

Gerard and the woman turn around and stare.

"Right up there," Orel continues, pointing at the hillside, "in what used to be the sculpture studio."

This was an artist community before the contaminations, where the peaceniks lived and made their folk art, commuting to well-paying jobs in the city. Lucas's parents took him here when he was a kid, to look at the pottery and the wild totems made by bearded software engineers and university professors. Gerard is stroking his beard, much like Lucas remembers the artisans of yore doing, as he gazes off where the boy is pointing.

"That geodesic," Gerard says slowly, in a different tone now, "is where you want to build a salmon farm? Because you think you can put freshwater tanks in there, which would sustain salmon farming."

Lucas rattles off a list of components he would need to construct a large tank for aquaculture of salmon. Many of the materials are close by; all he needs is two weeks to have it up and running.

"Where would you get the original spawn?" the woman asks, lifting her eyebrows into the dirty cap on her head.

Lucas points to the trunk of his car.

"We made a stop at a hatchery on the way in," he says. "I have a friend."

The youngest of the men steps forward and introduces himself as Kione, the leader of this community. He waves Orel to come around the car and shakes his hand. His smile is full of white teeth, which is rare, since red wine supplements for so many, and his handshake pumps their arms almost to the point of exhaustion.

"So you know where you are then?" Kione says in a friendly tone, stepping back with a grin.

"It used to be known as 'Bynum,'" replies Lucas.

Kione thrusts his hand in his denim pockets and looks around, chin jutted so that his yellow beard flaps in the wind. He takes a long, as-if-for-the-first-time look around the hamlet, with its post-war houses and their skinny frames, wide porches and derelict lawns.

"It's home." Kione smiles so that his eyes crinkle. "Where you are, Mr. Fishfarm, is *home.*"

He tells them to leave their things in the car, except for the crate of salmon fingerlings, which he and Gerard will tote across the river (they do not call it a stream). The newcomers drop behind the group as they walk across the beaten bridge. Orel goes along the edge, looking over at the churning waters as they collide with boulders and fold into slate-gray sloughs, limbs poking out here and there, and far off there is a bittern on careful legs looking upriver to a noisy falls.

The woman, Nan, turns around and spits, her eyes catching the boy's.

"If I had to guess," she says kindly, "I would say you haven't gone fishing in a while."

Orel looks at his father, who nods his head.

"Well, you've come to the right place, then," she chuckles.

*   *   *

They have dinner at Gerard's house, a rambling five-bedroom he shares with Nan and their three sons, all redheads with shining green eyes who each have their own shepherd dogs. The dogs' personalities are eerily like the boys'—even tempered and curious, proud in a quiet way. The oldest boy is Orel's age, and he invites Orel to his room to talk about cameras and photography. There are photos pinned to the pine walls throughout the house, mostly details of plants and insects, with a few portraits of long-nosed Gerard and Nan's definitely Irish mug.

"We're a hot chocolate-type family," Nan is saying as she turns a stew in a gigantic copper pot on her wood stove, which is the size of a small car. "We sit around the fireplace there and tell stories and talk shop until the dogs start howling for their walks."

Lucas asks why the dogs don't live outdoors, considering all the miles of woodlands and riverbeds, the starry nights and fresh open air.

"People eat dogs nowadays," she says, tasting her deer stew from the tip of her thumb. "It's what they call 'string barbecue' out here. You'd be amazed what you can eat if you close your mind to the taboos of yesteryear."

Lucas tells her of the bizarre culinary feats pulled off over barrel fires in the city, not just rats and pigeons, but babies. Like the case with that young woman by the bank who was looking to sell off a dead infant.

"I cringe to think about that," Nan hisses, looking around for Gerard, who has gone off to do something in the cellar and hasn't returned. "We hear the stories about what happens in the city. The boys bring home all sorts of mess from school. Underground tunnels where drug cultures flourish in dark ecosystems, maimings in broad daylight right in front of the capitol, and whole neighborhoods being burned out by our own soldiers. It is all too horrible to imagine being real."

He tells her it is quite real, explaining the hut city by the reservoir, which must be the inspiration for the tale of burned-out neighborhoods. She shakes her head the whole time. Gerard has come up the stairs and is washing his hands in the sink while she updates him on life in the city.

"Unacceptable," Gerard sighs, turning to look at Lucas. "Why didn't you and your son get out sooner?"

Lucas shrugs. One can get locked. He had a great job in a time of almost half unemployment. They seemed to stay closer to Sila, even if just to their memory of her, by living there.

"Your wife is dead?" Nan asks.

Lucas nods, sips at his coffee.

"Someone torched our house one day," he explains quietly. "She got locked inside. Maybe she was just asleep and never woke up during the fire. But she burned in it. They identified her by her teeth."

Gerard sits across from him at the table and gazes out the darkening kitchen windows. He says his father died in a robbery on the highway, returning from the mountains. The old man had been photographing the waterfalls in the Pisgah forest, documenting them for magazines. Just after his truck eased out of the hills, he stopped for gas and they jumped him and cut off his head with a chainsaw.

"And these were the religious people," Gerard says angrily, squeezing his mug so hard Lucas fears it might break. "Not some meth-fueled criminal cult, but a bunch of Christians who wanted to send a message back east: Stay away, we're full up with people here."

"His mother went crazy," Nan whispers, setting plates on their little high table. "She's still here, but not here, you know? That's where Gerard was just now. She lives in the cellar, won't come out for nothing."

"She will go for weeks without speaking," Gerard adds. "And when she does, it's gibberish. They may as well have murdered her, for all that's left of her."

One of the boys bounds in with his dog at his heels, both making similar grunting noises, both aiming for a seat at the end of the big table off in the dining room.

"The boys seem normal and happy don't they?" Gerard says as his wife calls for the rest of the boys, instructing them *not* to bring their dogs to the table tonight. "But I wonder if they are. I mean, you can't really hide happy. Happy is happy, and they seem to be truly happy at times. I just don't know if they are normal, if there is a normal anymore. Sometimes I wonder if we're doing them any favors by raising them traditionally. Maybe it would be better just to go ahead and let the boys inherit some of this darkness that has such a grip on Mother Earth. Maybe that would be the more responsible thing to do."

Lucas stares at the long-nosed man, wondering right along with him. It is a fine ethical dilemma, for which he has absolutely no answers. It is the type of thing he has discussed with Juda countless times over the past few years, finding neither conclusion nor resolution.

"Happy trumps normal," he says finally. "At least you and Nan and your boys have that."

6.

Orel and the oldest boy, Nico, take off into the hillside woods through paths made hard and smooth over the years. Nico is rangy like his father, and he swings up the trail by guiding with a long walnut pole. They stop at a ridge overlooking the falls, which is nothing more than a wide eight-foot-tall dam. Nico pulls out his camera and shoots for a moment. It is an old model and has a noisy shutter.

Orel crouches just below him, swings his lens and captures a peacenik in the wild, observing nature. Nico's face is round and smooth, his eyes large, and green with a grayish cast—like sage.

"You put your stuff on the boards?" Nico asks after frowning perfectly for Orel's portrait. Orel says there are three or four chains where people go a lot, especially Europeans and people on the West Coast. He says the best places, the ones you have to hunt for if you don't know somebody who can tell you where they are, are almost right there in plain sight.

"It's illegal to document a lot of things," Nico says, surveying the trail below. Often there is a deer or a raccoon that has come by and left tracks. He wants to show Orel some of these.

"It's illegal to drive a car more than fifty miles in one day," Orel replies. "But people still do it."

Nico says he thinks it won't be long before all laws are ceremonial and nobody abides by them. He holds up his hand to stop Orel.

"I know it's already like that out there. But I mean in all things, including the government and the military."

Orel looks out over the misty Haw and watches a blue heron glide around a bend and disappear. He takes more shots, since it is starting to drizzle and Nico says they may have to turn back soon. There are a few clans of citoyens around, but not the worst types. Just lazy, Nico says. They would rather steal than work for something.

There is a twisted line of black smoke just to the west, which Nico says is a camp of about fifty citoyens. He says a lot of them got a bad deal from the government way back before, an agreement to allow them to live—however crudely—on public lands. His father doesn't think it is a pact that should still be followed. Gerard says the citoyens should rebel.

"Good luck with that," Orel chuckles, wiping his camera and stuffing it back in his bag. He pulls out a granola bar and takes a bite.

Nico shrugs. His father is an idealist, and it may be the idealists who bang some sense back into the world. But then again, there's Nan's point of view: When you go past the point of no return, at some point there's nothing to return to.

"Your mom is the pessimist?" Orel says, watching the riverbed trails for some of the animals that Nico and his brothers say pass along it all day and night. Nico grins.

"She's just a hardass," he says. "She was in the Navy before she met my dad."

They descend slowly, careful of their footing around snaky root systems, pocketing pawpaw fruit as they go, until they reach the black, bubbly swirl of the dam. Nico says his mother has instructed him to teach Orel how to properly fish.

"But I'm not going to," Nico says as he tosses a stone into the eddy. "It's pretty boring stuff. You just tell her that we fished and that I taught you like a champ."

They stand on a catwalk over the spillway and listen to the steady soft roar of the water. To Orel, it sounds like a hundred industrial heaters all running at once. The river swells in the distance, twisting as it approaches, and something drifts their way in slow promenade to the falls. It is a pale body below the surface, with an arm thrusting out, fist tightened around a smoldering stick. Orel watches the body—it looks like a huge dead fish, except for the submerged legs—as it spins between stones and gapes eyeless to the fresh rain now falling in earnest.

"What was that?" asks Orel. "That ... that thing had been dead for a while. Why was it holding some torch that had just gone out?"

Nico leads the way back to his house, moving even slower on the now muddy trail.

"Is it a warning?" Orel asks, though Nico still hasn't said anything. Nico uses his pole to turn and offer his city friend a hand.

"We don't know what that is," Nico says when they top the ridge, back above the house again and its comforting yellow windows and chimney smoke. "But it's the type of thing that happens more and more often, which makes people think this is a haunted valley. In essence, it's what keeps us safe, Orel."

* * *

Gerard helps Lucas lug all the pipes and fittings into the empty geodesic. Several of the other men from the roadside encounter also help. But not Kione. He is, to Lucas, conspicuous in his absence. So, as they fasten together the walls of an old aboveground swimming pool, he asks Gerard about the status with Kione. He looks awful young to be a leader of this community and all its graybeards.

Gerard smiles and motions through a window for the water to be turned on.

"He's something of a genius, where security is concerned," he tells Lucas. "He's a kid, per se, but he's fearless and he came to us with invaluable experience."

He motions out the window to cut the water. There is a trickle between two of the steel walls.

"He came from the city like you," Gerard says, looking at Lucas now. "He was chief of security at the military prison. A special forces guy. A trained killer. But he'd had enough and wanted out. Through a friend of a friend of a friend, he found his way here."

Gerard signals through the window, water back on.

"Kione keeps the mood upbeat," he continues as water gushes in and the walls hold dry this time. "He knows how to handle intruders. He's not afraid of resorting to violence."

Inwardly, Lucas worries about anybody who comes from the military prison. Its reputation is the worst. Kione may have had enough, but likely not before he committed some atrocious acts of his own. Lucas has learned that you do not always return intact from your misdeeds. Parts of him are scattered all over the city and its once-shady suburbs. His silences, all those times he saw directives pulsing through the Public Vita that he knew were shrouded in the cruelest secrets, plotting downfalls and the slow, steady genocide of the citoyens. How many times had he said nothing?

Gerard signals to go ahead and release the fingerlings into the tank. He has promised this water—drawn from the bubbly tidal pools of a downriver stream—is uncontaminated. He proved it by drinking a glass first thing this morning, wiping his lips with a broad smile.

Lucas climbs a ladder and removes the bladder from the crate, then empties the bladder into the tank. Thousands of silvery salmon dart inside the murky pool. There is barely a ripple on the surface after only a few seconds.

"We're salmon farmers now," Lucas grins, looking around the room to assure all that this is a moment they should capsulate and commit to memory. He climbs down and switches on the purifier he has rigged up for these adventures in aquaculture. It purrs on and soon the tank is effervescent with an environment suitable for growing tens of thousands of Coho.

"Anybody know how to cook a good salmon?" he asks as they start heading for the door. One of the older men pauses just outside, rain dripping from his mustache, and catches Lucas as he goes by. The man's hand is like a steel clamp upon his arm and he whispers into his ear before Lucas has a chance to react.

"Have you seen them?" he asks. "Have you been to the church?"

Lucas looks around but the others have all continued walking away, including Gerard.

"We're supposed to move into the church tonight," he tells the jumpy graybeard. "My son and I."

The old man shakes his head ruefully. He wags a bent yellow finger under Lucas's nose. His eyes seem to crackle with misspent enthusiasm.

"It's haunted by the worst souls," he warns.

Lucas nods and pats the elderly fellow on his shoulder.

"I've heard all about it," he says kindly. "Gerard is going to hook me up with a ghost-away machine. My son and I will have them out and on their way to heaven or hell in no time."

The old man stops and gives Lucas a look of disgust. He looks away, spits, and stands there with rainwater dripping off his old beaten fedora.

"Moron," the old man mutters before walking off in the other direction, toward one of the smallest huts down the hill.

Later, he asks Gerard about this guy, this mossback with his peculiar views on the paranormal. Gerard admits the fellow is backwards. But he is from one of the old Bynum families, a man by the name of Eddie Drake who is truly harmless but obviously a little shaded by outdated spirituality and beliefs.

"Kione calls him 'Hocus Pocus.' It's an apt name, don't you think?"

Lucas nods and tries to think of the last time he met such an old-timer, someone who seemed to have a direct connection to the world before. He has vague memories of his great-grandfather, a man with wiry gray hair in his nose and ears, who shook so badly it affected his speech. This ancestor seemed to talk of entire days at the seaside, roasting oysters and laying in the sun ... or driving to work on sunny freeways, bumper-to-bumper traffic, taking the kids to crowded malls on the weekends. If there were a ghost involved in any of this, it would be Lucas's memory.

"It is a good name for him," Lucas smiles.

* * *

It's the Friday night meeting for Gail and his brethren. They gather in a basement room to discuss defectors, crimes— all the things that provide those like Gail a chance to commune with violence. These are division heads, random spies with federal ties, the members of an inner circle that has so badly lost its way, it has no idea where it's going anymore. There is only one desired outcome, Gail tells a tall, dark-skinned man from the North who suffers from a constant, muffled cough.

For years their predecessors sat in legislative buildings and drafted laws that conflicted with the basic human order. One of the first was to forgo elections and only have appointed governments, yet they still called it a democracy. Revolutions arose, on a variety of scales, as the electorate lost their grip on national politics and then across the states and cities and towns. Corporations boldly armed this new leadership. They found ways to violently stifle the final writhing legacies of constitutional democracy. Old men shuffled into these tunneled rooms and branded the new government this and that—functional democracy, military democracy, secular democratic republic for here and there, until it was everywhere.

In the end, they left it in shambles, once it was so broken it couldn't work. They called everything the same thing as before, saluted the constitutions of all governments, and yet secretly changed it all. There was no record of what they did.

The Northern man taps a cigarette into his palm and considers Gail's complaint. He is known for scuttling vital water operations in one area to benefit another, based on potentials. He has shut down purification plants in much of the Piedmont, all of the coast, and Gail believes he is here now to shut down the central purifying system. This man has a daughter in isolation, put there because he felt she could no longer be trusted.

"Do you have a light?" the man asks, coughing.

Gail does not smoke. He says one of the others, a Transportation official, should be along soon. While they wait, the Northern man acts dissatisfied.

"One of your scientists left?" he says finally. "Can you track him?"

Gail says the scientist, Lucas, left his tracking wire behind.

"You didn't wire his car?"

"He didn't take his car. I don't think he owns one."

The Northern man frowns, strokes his upper lip and closes his eyes. He is like a breathing sculpture. He smells of cigarettes and wet wool.

"It's about to happen, Gail," he says, coughing softly at the end, his eyes closing.

"I suspected it couldn't be long."

"We've concluded we have no way out."

Gail nods. "There's no reason for us to doubt our choices."

"This isn't a choice." The Northern man opens his eyes as footsteps come along the corridor. He looks at Gail.

"Yes, that's him," Gail says.

The Northern man gets a light from the Transportation official, watches him trail down the dark hallway, and looks down at the floor. Stars were painted there years ago, before the new way. There are silvery traces—outlines—of the points of each star.

"I have to ask if you are prepared for this," the Northern man says, dropping ashes on the floor. They look at the ashes together, each one wondering if the other sees the brief image of a world turned to ashes by nuclear holocaust.

"Yes," Gail says. He has never even tried to have his engineers and scientists, even the bright ones such as Lucas, devise an exit strategy, any alternative to holocaust. "We've been coming to this for a while now."

The man shakes his head. His eyes turn a little sad.

"This seems something like you would want, Gail. And there are others. I'm not one of those, the ones like you. Not this time. Not to this extreme. I am on the side of humanity in this case, although it's not the winning side."

"Humanity always loses," Gail says.

"Yes we do," the Northern man says. He drags hard on his cigarette and erupts into a fit of hacks and snorts.

* * *

Nico looks at his electronic images on a review screen, a refrigerator-sized sheet of white laminate stuck to his wall with construction adhesive. They got his digital projector from one of the old peaceniks who was leaving to take his wife up North.

He displays photo after photo onto the homemade screen, and he and Orel critique each other, sometimes laughing at a tilted accidental frame, then quietly peering into one person's view of a landscape, an opaque window, and the slice of a profile as it comes to rest before the aperture.

Orel gasps at some of his friend's work with nature. There are crawly bugs and creepy reptiles, shaved cottontails blurring last year's solar flare, and tiny waterfalls from the surrounding stony nooks and unkempt meadows, just a vast bursting display of what remains intact.

"You are so lucky," Orel sighs. His heart is absolutely pounding with ... he is not sure what, but his excitement is hard to contain.

Nico smiles and puts up Orel's shots from the dam. They are bleak, but that is his style. Nico says it is because he is urban, and the city has become so grim. They are looking at a glassy image of water with a gray shoreline when something catches Nico's eye. He jumps off his bed and runs to the wall, practically puts his nose into the light.

"There!" he says. "What's *that*?"

Orel goes up but he can't see anything out of the ordinary. It is water and sand and trees. And, well, maybe there is a ... a fleck of white cloth ... perhaps it is a person ... a man standing on the shore looking directly at the photographer ... a man with a long face and a scraggly beard ... and silver-shining eyes.

Orel puts his hand over his mouth and turns around.

"What? Who is that guy? Do you know him or something?"

Orel nods. He sits on the bed and then lays back and stares at the ceiling. His head is spinning and his heart is racing faster than before, only now with dread—not excitement.

"He's the intruder from the city," Orel says without emotion.

He tells his father about it, when they are unpacking their things in the church. They have been given a few pieces of furniture to get them going, along with ample supplies for the kitchen, which is back behind the apse. They are stowing dishes and coffee mugs when Orel describes his photograph. Lucas pauses, plate in hand, and stares at the pine counter. Then he goes over and starts unloading their cutlery.

"Aren't you going to say anything?" Orel says, a little panicky. "Aren't you worried at all, Dad?"

Lucas folds the empty boxes neatly and slides them under the sink. He takes a stack of towels out of his son's hands and tosses them onto the counter. Then he folds his arms over his chest, tilts his head approvingly, and looks blankly at the boy.

"I am always worried," he says. "I have been in a constant state of worry since the day you were born. I don't expect I will ever have a day without worries. But they have this guy Kione here, who is something of an assassin or an executioner, maybe both. I think our intruder will have to worry about him, should he come strolling into town. And then we have our ghosts."

"Ghosts?"

"Yeah, we've got ghosts on our side of the bridge," Lucas says as he goes over to the window and peers across the nighttime landscape at the hillside, on the other side of the river, where glowing windows and smoky flues glow cheerily from within the darkness.

"Didn't Nico tell you our church is haunted?"

Orel shrugs and looks around the well-lit kitchen. Lucas can tell what he's thinking.

"It is very haunted," Lucas laughs. Then he goes out into the sanctuary where he has rigged the Dolby to play directly from Orel's button. And there, in their new, spectral home in a house of God on the river's edge, Lucas loudly plays the opening flourishes of *Toccata and Fugue in D Minor* for any and all to hear.

7.

Strange things happen in the night. One of Orel's (now deceased) classmates used to have this tattooed on his shoulder. It was accompanied by a leering, bald vampire with teeth oozing a smoky paste. The kid lived a few blocks from their house in a massive Tuscan with colonnades that should have been given their own zoning.

Orel thinks of him as he tries to fall asleep the first night in the church. Nobody ever called the kid by his real name. He was a couple years older than most in the class, which Orel thinks was seventh grade. The past is fuzzy, but so is the present. He went by "Auggie" and was tall and muscled but had a limp of some kind, affecting his left leg. Or maybe it was his right.

He would show the tattoo to anyone who asked to see it. It had plenty of color in the vampire head, unlike so many that you see now. Orel used to draw pictures of it in his notebooks, secretly plotting to have it stamped on his own body somewhere. But then Auggie turned up dead one morning, right by the school, and put a damper on those plans.

"I see all sorts of things at night," Auggie used to say, darting his eyes around in case anyone he didn't want to hear was trying to eavesdrop. He liked to say, "listen here, mates" as a sort of opening for all of his tales, and it always preceded his ghost stories.

"My mum says there are people in the walls," he whispered to Orel as they stood in a hallway line one winter morning. "Blokes who got themselves murdered for one reason or another."

And then Auggie got murdered himself. Decapitated. Body dumped right there by the playing fields for all the students to see as they streamed off the buses one morning. One kid picked up Auggie's frozen head and threw it toward a net, as if it was the ball in an ongoing game.

"I have hallucinations," Auggie said just days before he was murdered. "I can't for the life of me stop having them. It's like someone is putting them in my brain, and I feel like it's these ghosts who are doing it. They just won't stop. My mum thinks I'm crazy and wants to cram me in an asylum."

This was when Orel discovered he was gay, and Auggie was the first boy Orel ever fell in love with.

Orel thumbs through a rumpled paperback he found in the top of his closet, a sort of history of the old town Bynum and its "notable places," including this church. An Episcopal church built around the Civil War, it became home to evangelicals in the 1970s, and most recently was a refuge for thumpers on their way to the mountains. Its lineage is rather unimpressive, Orel decides.

But what is interesting are the moons and stars lacquered inside all the closets and vestibules. "Never let this darkness keep you," someone has written, also in phosphorescent paint, on the back wall of his closet. He wonders if someone, the author perhaps, was locked in this closet to protect him from something evil, or maybe it was the reverse—the author was far too evil to run loose as he pleased. His imagination is going full steam.

He hears his father doing something with their food in the kitchen downstairs. He imagines him storing the root vegetables in a dark pantry, rewrapping meats for daily usage, washing greens so that they can have salad tomorrow. Lucas is whistling, the happiest he has been in some time. It is a song they used to play, Lucas and Sila, in the living room of their old house, the one that burned. The music was some instrumental version of an ancient love song that his mother would sing, laughing whenever her husband tried to join in.

And now, Lucas warbles his old line, his eyes closed and his mouth twisted in fake agony. But there is no one to laugh at him anymore, nobody to shush him because he is singing the wrong verse and interrupting her long full notes of the last "goodbye" in the song. He is sobbing at the sink now, wiping his face with a towel and staring blearily into darkness. It has been nine years. There is nothing he can do to stop it once it starts.

There is a sound outside, some kind of bird. It makes a noise that is both a low call and a snort. Nico and Gerard warned them both that waterfowl here are nocturnal noisemakers.

Orel listens to the melancholy bird. Its lament breaks an otherwise deep silence, like clockwork, every half a minute. Then it stops and the unbroken hush returns. The only sound is from within the church, where Lucas grieves quietly for his dead wife.

* * *

During the night, Orel dreams of a desert where shadowy men in black balloon pants are shaving at an oasis, discussing peculiar events such as bridal parties where jackals feasted on roses and cognac, and volcanoes that sprang open and gushed lava onto deserted cities. The men laugh at everything and have little sense of comedy. The mere fact that one of the youngest cannot find blades for his razor throws them all into prolonged guffaws.

He awakens at the first shades of a blue dawn and is so thirsty he thinks he may have swallowed fire, providing a lingering reminder of his dream. But it's just the heating in the church; the fireplace at the end of the hall (a strange place to put one, even his father said so) lets off tremendous heat. And there is a hot, dry breeze that rises from downstairs, from the direction of the sanctuary, which is almost perfumed.

He makes coffee in the kitchen and watches the brightening of the east. The woods on the tops of distant hills are leafless and dark, in a calming way. There is a flush of pale just below the peak of one hill, a lonely arc without houses or huts or the sprawling wires of livestock pens. It moves like a ghost against a difficult terrain, with lurches and stops, seeming to hover almost in the limbs of black locust trees. Orel watches with drowsy fascination until he realizes all at once that this arboreal phantom takes the form of the intruder from professor's house, who has climbed a tree to spy on this church. Within those bare limbs he can view the church, from foundation to steeple. He moves only when the cold wind shakes the woods.

Orel looks around for the switch and when he looks back to the hill the man is gone from his tree. As he scans for more signs of the man it begins to snow, lightly at first, dissolving on the glass. But before he can clear the fog of his breath from the glass it has changed to a furious downpour of wet spring flakes. Nearby chickens launch into a bedlam as a goat runs past the churchyard, down the muddy hill into a thicket of berry bushes where it can only be heard for its frantic bleating.

The boy lowers his head to the counter to get away from this phantasmagoria, to gather his wits and reason if this outlaw has indeed followed them from the city. He makes more coffee for his father, who will get up soon. He pulls on his wet gear, grabs his camera bag, and sneaks out the red front doors to head over to Nico's. He figures between the two of them they can come up with something.

* * *

Nico takes him down into the cellar. His grandmother's smell is pungent—not offensive, but actually somewhat intoxicating, like powders and perfumes that exist only in rare instances now. Orel expects creaky stairs but they are firm, poured concrete, and wide enough for you to haul down furniture or appliances. Nico explains this was a bunker that the previous owner built.

"Not all the peaceniks are safe from paranoia," he says.

At the bottom, Nico pulls a chain and a row of bulb lights comes on. It is one enormous open room with woven rugs littering the stone floor. There is a kitchenette to the right, with a flickering fluorescent bulb that glows blue over a counter stacked with hand-painted dinnerware, and a nook cookery where Nan sometimes prepares small meals.

"She cooks sometimes," Nico whispers, looking around for his reclusive grandmother, who seems to be in the enclosed lavatory in the back, just to the right of a screened bed. It is an old four-poster surrounded by several tables and lamps.

They go to the front screen and Nico drags it open quietly, pointing at the heaps of paperbacks on the tables.

"Ghost stories," he whispers, grinning. "Can you imagine?"

It is less like a tomb and more like the lair for some eccentric magnate or an archaic professor being shielded from political persecution. The lavatory toilet flushes.

"We're in here, Granna," Nico calls out. He scuffs at the floor with his shoes and looks at his friend and shrugs. The lock clicks and out shuffles a tiny, frail woman who is wrapping a scarf around her bald head. She has a long nose like Gerard's, and a pointy chin that she buries in her chemise. She smiles faintly.

Nico introduces Orel and he puts out his hand, but the woman tiptoes toward her bed, sits on her mattress, lifts huge cat glasses to her nose, and stares at him.

"Pretty," she says, her voice phlegmy and Southern, a lilt that has all but vanished. She waves toward a table where her teacup sits still nearly full with orange pekoe. Her grandson ferries it over nervously, standing beside the bed and waiting while she sips. She passes the cup to Nico when she is done and goes back to staring at Orel. She reminds him of a teacher at the school who used to make students wipe their shoes before entering her class.

"What is she supposed to tell us?" Orel asks when they are at the sink so Nico can rinse out the teacup and put it on a shelf lined with pressed linen. The purpose of their visit with the old woman in the cellar is baffling to Orel. Nico just puts a finger to his lips.

His grandmother is already asleep, reading glasses on her chest, mouth parted so that her breathing can be heard rasping through her weak lungs. Nico motions him to follow, and now they are tiptoeing through the screens, exiting out the other side to a shadowy corner that holds a massive armoire that is at least two-hundred years old. Nico pops the doors open silently and starts rummaging around. He bends down and then comes back up to re-inspect the top shelves.

"Aha!" he whispers, folding something in a cloth and jamming it into his pocket. He motions to Orel that they should leave now. They pass the sleeping crone, straighten the screens, switch off the lights and scurry up the concrete steps like long-legged mice.

On the other side of the door Nan is waiting with a frown. Not the look of typical motherly consternation, though, because her eyes are wet and she is patting a tissue at her pointy nose.

"Your brothers' dogs are dead," she says hoarsely. "Both of them."

She sits down at the kitchen table. She wipes at her eyes furiously, and her lips move but nothing comes out. Then she looks at them.

"Both of them killed and left out by the wood shed. Blows to the head. And they were such good dogs, such beautiful shepherds …"

Nan gives into her hysterics now, throwing her arms in the air and slapping her hands hard on the wood., shaking all the condiments in the center.

8.

The young brothers are standing at the woodshed, hands in coat pockets and their breaths streaming, discussing what to do. The youngest, Cyril, takes a shovel from the edge of the stack and goes up the hill to start digging graves.

"Whoever did it," says the other one, a long-haired redhead named Torrey, "just left them out here for the bobcats to get. They weren't killed to be eaten by men."

Nico nods his head and squats beside the dogs, a pair of sisters who were about to turn five and had become adept scouts on long hiking trips. Cyril called his Belle, and Torrey called his Bella. It looks like Bella was slain first, since the blow to her head is the only mark on her. Belle seems to have given a fight, perhaps seeking revenge for the murder of her sister. There are lacerations along her nose and above her right eye, meaning it took numerous strikes to bring her down.

"Bella was killed when somebody dropped a stone on her head," Nico says after a while. "And I think Belle came after him but he had a weapon, like a hammer or something. Maybe we should look around later, once the dogs are buried, to see if anything is out there."

He looks up at Orel.

"I definitely think your intruder is out there," he says coldly, "and he is still doing bad things."

Cyril comes loping down the hill, out of breath, so sweaty that steam rises from his coat. He says the graves are dug and they should come on now. He and Torrey load the dogs into a wheelbarrow and they all take turns pushing it up the wet, rocky hillside.

Between two tall white ash trees they see twin holes, and a pile of stones that Cyril removed during the dig, that will mark the dogs' graves. Torrey spills some powdered lime into the graves, and they wrap Belle and Bella in burlap before placing them in their graves. The younger boys quickly shovel the loamy soil back in and Nico stamps around on the mounds afterwards.

Torrey mutters a few words and then directs Cyril to step up and do the same. He leans on his shovel like a veteran gravedigger, chewing on his fingernails. He shakes his head and lets them know there is nothing to say. He just wants to get back to the house and have something to eat and warm up with some hot chocolate.

"It hasn't sunk in yet," little Cyril says woefully. "It won't seem like it's happened till I run down to the river next time and Belle isn't all between my legs the whole way."

He wags his head and removes his cap to wipe at his soggy hair.

"It's a sorry scoundrel who done this," he says.

*   *   *

You can spend all day watching the tank and it's like you can *feel* the salmon growing, Lucas has been telling Gerard and Kione. They are all on scaffolding around the aquaculture rig, peering in like children at the zoo. The water bubbles nicely, soothingly, and Lucas dips his fingertips in and scoops them along.

"How'd you keep it like this?" he asks as Kione lights a cigarette and turns his back to the tank. "Nobody can keep fresh water now. Nobody. It can't be done. I heard rumors. We all heard rumors. But rumors are like your nose."

"Everybody's got one?" grins Kione as he flicks ashes out onto the wet floor.

Gerard leans out over the water and scoops at it like Lucas. He smells his fingers and shrugs.

"The old people have their tricks," he says. "They say put this ditch here, that ditch there, stack some rocks here, and cut back some cattails there. Your mossback friend? Old Drake? He knows a lot. There are a lot of his ideas going into cleaning our water supply."

"Go figure that," Lucas sighs. He is interested in what Kione is doing, which looks like nothing. The guy is just combing out his ponytail, but there is something brewing in his mind. You can see the cogs turning.

"You would think people would stampede this place for our water, right?" Gerard continues. "That they'd come and stand in line with jugs and buckets to get theirs purified. But they don't and it's because there's a consensus around that this is haunted land. Evil spirits and all that."

Kione laughs and flicks his cigarette butt at the steel wall, where it bursts into countless sparks. He glances at Lucas and turns back to the tank. He dips his fingers, in imitation of Lucas and Gerard, but it doesn't hold the same fascination to him.

"You ever visit the military prison in the city, Lucas?" he asks, with perfect nonchalance. In the old days, he would have made a successful car salesman or a terrifically cunning CIA interrogator. Lucas says he hasn't, but he's heard stories.

"Ghost stories," Kione chuckles, stroking his yellow beard, which he has taken to tying off at the end with a rubber band. "This is all we have in our world now, ghost stories. Such awful and wonderful tales. It seems everybody has one and if they don't—they get one. You know what? I remember hearing my grandfather talk about God. Capital G God. The big boy God, with all his wrath and the thunderous revenge and a host of heavenly angels in his choir. A God you could count on, and likewise a God you couldn't count on for nothing."

Lucas looks at Gerard and Gerard looks away. Kione keeps going.

"There used to be a million ways to piss God off. It didn't take much. You remember? God was everywhere and in all things, and if you said otherwise, they would cut you down to size real fast. Swift and vengeful. Vengeful and swift. Kinda romantic, all in all. Put a smile on a lot of faces."

He looks at Lucas with emotionless eyes.

"And a lot of pain and woe in some others. You get what I'm talking about, Mr. Lucas?"

Lucas nods faintly, hoping Kione will not ask him to elaborate.

"I used to lie in the barracks at night and wonder what happened to God," the ex-soldier continues, smoothing the cuffs of his sleeves like a businessman would. "It kept me awake, if you can believe it. But I never came to a conclusion, just never got there. There was a dead end with me, where good is concerned, moral goodness or whatever name you have for it. We should get it from God, right? Pumped into our veins like a drug. If we have evil, and we do, then we must have good."

Kione lights another cigarette and stares into the water as if he knows what he is looking at in there, as though he's been farming fish all his life.

"But I don't see it, Lucas. I've looked for it for years and I did not find it. Thus, if we are devoid of benevolence, then this caring good God does not exist. Likely never did. It was just all a bunch of rotten ghost stories, if you ask me."

He turns his head left and right, catching shimmers of salmon smolt in the middle depths.

"How much salmon will this produce in a week?" he asks Lucas.

"One-hundred pounds, give or take."

"Every week?"

"Like clockwork."

Kione scratches his beard and looks past Lucas, at Gerard.

"That'll make the goats happy," he says to the herder, a thin smile twitching on his lips.

* * *

Gerard comes around to the church at dusk, broken up over the death of his son's dogs. He's rattled, so he brings a bottle of bourbon with him to sit down and share with the newcomers. He says Nan would have come, but she's too furious to leave the house.

"I think she's already three sheets as well," the tall man smiles, raising his glass to Lucas and Orel. He is sluggish in his movements, and Lucas gets the feeling Nan isn't the only drunk one.

"The last dog, Bixby, Nico's shepherd, just keeps howling," mutters Gerard. "Can you hear it? It's all we can hear over there. Just nonstop all around the outside of the house, circling the house slowly, keening in his own endless way."

Lucas puts his hand over his glass when Gerard tries to pour him more.

"It's driving the old lady crazy. My mother, not Nan. She's in bad shape because of it. I've tried talking to her to calm her down, but it's like talking to a stone."

Gerard sloshes his glass full again. When Lucas turns his head to cough, he gets a refill halfway to the rim. The way people drink now, there is nothing unusual about this. Distilleries were once a widely scattered industry, but now they populate like supermarkets. People make their own as they can, since the process bypasses the chronic water problems. Lucas worked with a woman years ago who said she cooked her rice in sake, and her potatoes with cheap champagne.

"What *exactly* is wrong with her?" Lucas asks.

Gerard waves his hand in the air and sighs. He has blocky tattoos on his fingers' middle knuckles, Japanese symbols in heavy blue, and the emblems for the Communist Party on the backs of his hairy hands. They are the fading marks of a much younger man.

"Post-traumatic stress disorder, according to doctors. But she was a live wire, emotionally, before my father was killed." Gerard takes a long drink and stares at his again-empty glass. "You can't take the crazy out of crazy, right? But, look, she has a right to be like she is. She has every damned right."

Lucas says nobody is disputing that.

"My father's head showed up on our porch one day. Did I tell you that? Delivered in the post. Box was tied with twine, packaged real nice. We thought it was a sympathy gift from relatives. So we brought it over to the sofa—one of those wingback deals with floral designs all over it—and sat down and, for the first time in days, acted cheerful."

He takes a drink straight from the bottle and then realizes what he's doing. He holds it out for requests but there are no takers this time. Lucas excuses himself and goes over to the stove to check on Orel's red bean stew. He's stirring a wooden spoon around the pot when Gerard continues.

"So we're preparing to each go 'ooh' and 'ahh' when she finally gets it open, but it doesn't go that way. But you knew that. We are hanging our faces over the box when she pries the lid off and there's a browned head—the color you see on canyon walls, in pictures out west in Arizona or New Mexico—tilted back so that it's kind of looking up at us, surprised to see us a bit, if you want to go that far. And she just slaps the lid back on and presses her lips together and looks at me. I've got tears all in my eyes, so what I see is a blurry mother sitting there, turning to face me, and her mouth pops open—a black hole circled in red—and she says something. I will never forget what she says."

Like most drunks, Gerard makes them wait while he takes a long dramatic swig. He even wipes his mouth with the back of his hand like a cowboy.

"You know what she says?"

"The beans are almost ready," Lucas tells Orel.

"No," Gerard snaps. "There was nothing about beans. But you know what she said to me right then? She said, 'I've had enough.'"

Gerard looks around for reaction and seems satisfied when they bow their heads in sympathy.

"*I've had enough*. And then she hardly comes out of her own head for thirty years. A person can just decide they've had enough or hit their limit, and they can just guilt-free shut it down, take the rest of the game off. I don't get it. I was fourteen. I was just getting started."

"I'm sorry," he adds, wiping his nose. "You were just about to have dinner and I've interrupted long enough."

Lucas nods and escorts him to the kitchen door, throwing an arm around his shoulder as they go. Gerard is staggering a little now, and Lucas decides he will watch from the window to make sure he crosses the dark bridge safely.

"I hope I answered your question," he says in Lucas's ear.

"You did," Lucas says with a tap on his shoulder that is meant to guide Gerard safely to the top step.

9.

The last war was not a widespread affair, nor was it a holocaust or a series of surgical strikes on an embedded target. It was, as Kione tells Lucas, "a fifty-year extraction of teeth from a mummified theocracy." What he means by this is, with the decentralization of banks and the lost battles against environmental pollution, military forces were called upon to do less-than-heroic deeds.

They sit in the closest thing there is to sunshine now, on Gerard's expansive porch, and try to sort through the killing of the dogs and what Orel says are his sightings of the decrepit city intruder here in these woods.

"Religion matters most in pleasant times," Kione tells them. "We used to think just the opposite. The more dire it was, the more desperate we were for the kingdom of heaven. Right? Well, not exactly. Kind of a yes and no situation, if you want to know the truth. Yes for the people, no for the governments. There were a couple governments that fell back and wanted to spiritualize with the people. As things got bad all around, a nation or two wanted to stop and pray. So we neutralized them. Took them out to the ledge and hung 'em over by their ankles, if you will."

Gerard has a hangover and he sits in a rocking chair on the end of the porch with his eyes closed. The rest of them are fanned out, smoking and drinking coffee. The shepherd Bixby paces nervously in the front yard, sniffing wet stones and scanning the bare tree line up the hill where his sisters are buried.

"What I'm saying is," Kione continues, "this citoyen you have described to me, Lucas, is on the order of those leaders, the bureaucrats and chieftains of before, who were put down for the greater good. They didn't fear portents of peril for their disloyalty, and they damned sure didn't heed warning shots."

Lucas isn't sure what to think, other than to feel defeated by the realization that the city's evils have followed him and his son here. He has a sense that it is a sign that worse things are to come.

Kione tosses a pebble near the shepherd to get it to look away from wherever it is gazing off to. He looks down the row of bearded men to where Gerard sits motionless, asleep. He explains that if anyone meets this violator, their attempts to talk some sense into him will be futile. There should be no hesitation, no run-now-while-you-can speeches, nothing of that sort. Opportunity cannot be wasted.

"If you don't have a gun, get one. If you can't get one on your own, see me."

Lucas goes back to the church to tell his son what their orders are. Orel is unconvinced that he could shoot somebody, especially someone standing right in from of him. What if he misses or simply loses his nerve? And who is to say that this man won't have a gun himself?

"I thought we were going to set a trap, is all," he says disappointedly.

"Kione isn't about traps," Lucas says. "Kione is about shooting people in the head."

The bright sky does not last long, and around noon it starts to rain. Orel throws on a poncho and runs over to Nico's, hoping to brighten his friend's mood with a funny slideshow. He found the series just this morning. It is a hilarious stream of images of this kid who used to live down the street, who liked to drop his pants at passersby and ask for money. This was a little kid, somewhat brain damaged, who was shameless in his own special type of begging.

Nico smiles when he answers the door and tells his little brothers, still in quiet mourning for their dogs, that he will have to finish what they were doing later. Cyril waves a limp hand at Orel and Torrey is too busy screwing something into the back of the television to look up.

In Nico's room, they throw up the photos and laugh. The repulsive little citoyen flashes his rear end at a pair of high-lifers who, if Orel remembers correctly, roared with laughter and tossed a crumpled bill into his face. There is even a quick show of the ugly imp taking a dump on the curb, his swollen dirty face contorted as he pushes out feces.

"That's disgusting!" Nico bellows, falling back onto his bed. He puts his hand over his face and wheezes with delight. Orel flops down beside him, hands folded onto his chest, and his face turned to his friend. Nico slowly stops giggling and rolls his head to the side and stares at Orel. They are kissing when Nan comes banging on the door to announce that lunch is ready for whoever wants it.

* * *

Nico tells him the story of how his family came here, after World War II, via a Hell's Kitchen Irishman who had lost a hand in the Pacific while in the Navy. This great-great-grandfather was always talking about being a farmer, boring everybody in the city to death, and the people there were relieved when this bowlegged little kid was shipped out to the Solomon Islands.

Granpap Nick, Nico's namesake, served aboard a minesweeper that prowled for months at a time, as restless as a whore in church, the old man would say during his stories to Gerard and the grandchildren. They hit ports from Australia to the Bering Strait, sailing under the calmest rising moons and some of the strongest typhoons ever to slam through the Pacific.

Nick, who says the long night watches on deck cured him of being bowlegged, lost his hand in a bar fight in the Fiji Islands. It was, ironically, a cowboy bar with all the American Western themes—including posters of John Wayne and Randolph Scott—and a bunch of "crawly, oily Orientals" who eventually lost patience with the rowdy sailors.

The tale goes that Nick was knocked to the floor after he jumped on the back of two Fijians (likely untrue) and was coldcocked from behind by a fat German barmaid (sounds made up). A giant Aussie sat on his chest while some kind of weird Kung-Fu master chopped down with a katana and "de-handed your dear old Granpap Nick." It all sounds very fishy, but Nick came out of the Navy with an honorable discharge and a duffel bag filled with cash and vouchers. So he headed for North Carolina's ripe farmland and was traveling down Route 301, when he hung a hard right and ended up trying his hand (ha-ha) at fly fishing on the Haw River. Only there isn't any trout in the Haw and Nick got fed up and ready to leave when he bumped into a lovely Scottish damsel at a harvest dance, and they fell in love.

The bride's barley-brined parents bestowed the young couple a home on the banks of the Haw at Bynum and goat herders from miles around were soon in awe of Granpap Nick's herd, which produced milk and cheese at astonishing rates.

"Our goats are descendants of those goats," Nico says, taking a breath in the middle of his story. "They still put out more milk than any others I've ever seen."

Nick moved the family onto a larger farm in Chatham County, and kept the small rustic digs on the Haw for sport and rental income. That river house was later bought by a paranoid builder who installed a doomsday dungeon, which now is home to the grandmother. The builder eventually moved off, leaving it for Gerard to move back into, once Gerard was forced to abandon the sprawling farm in Chatham, as its water had become poisonous.

"We've come back home, so to speak," Nico says. "It wasn't a long move to get here. Dad says it took two days and would have only taken one if Granna hadn't freaked out. We had a cellar there."

Orel props himself on his elbow and closes his eyes. He tries to imagine what the oceans of before must have been like. Something akin to fresh beer is what he has been told. But you still couldn't drink it, even back then.

"I want to live in the North," he tells Nico quietly, as if it is something bad and should be kept a secret. "I'm trying to go to school there in the fall."

Orel listens to Nico's breathing, the soft pulls through the lungs that whisper back out through the nostrils, like a wind that goes all the way around the world and comes back gentler and more fragrant. He is in love and knows it's not the right thing to be doing. Not here and not now.

"You want to be a photographer?"

"A photojournalist."

"That's what I meant," Nico sighs. "You'll make a good one. One of the best."

They listen to the rain seeping against the cedar walls outside, sucking at the roots of sick trees that may have bloomed their last. Somewhere Bixby's tail is thumping against the porch boards.

"I want to make a difference," Orel says.

"I just want to be happy and live a long life," Nico says.

"I forgot what it's like to be happy."

"That's what my grandmother says. At least, according to my dad."

They listen again as the wind howls a bit, so that you can feel the house lean into it. The river is rising again and the stones disappear in the flowing torrents. They are thinking different things, like is seldom seen in new love, when the minds typically operate as one. They are counting the beautiful seconds that are going by, each like a raindrop in its own eternal storm.

"I want to be happy," Orel says at last.

* * *

Gail emerges from his concrete home every morning, one of the few of his order to go around unarmed. Gail is comfortable like this. There is always a soldier at the ready, just a tap on his button away. And he has a knife to handle thuggery, panhandlers, and even tricky doors.

The government food system amuses him. They deliver twice a week directly to his tiny kitchen. He notices the difference between the man and the woman who bring his food. The man always leaves the door rug slightly askew, as if he comes and goes roughly. There is often a cabinet door not entirely closed. The woman always leaves a faint scent behind, a Persian fragrance, somewhat musky but enticing. He has seen her, leaving hurriedly, her head down. A young woman, tall, graceful, a slash of electric blue in her hair—the cropped bangs that she brushes away before she climbs back into her rundown delivery truck.

He watches them, and others like them, from the black windows inside the train terminal (a secret viewing room for those like Gail), knowing who they are by the badges they show to board the westbound routes. There used to be more trains, more passengers, more happiness and indulgences. It used to be a tolerable world. There were goals to achieve that didn't require grave sacrifices at every turn. The disappearances were scarce, limited to those like Gail's grandfather—obvious traitors, the overly compassionate, and dissuaders of policy.

Now it's every other person you meet. They're marked secretly by a watcher, such as Gail, and coded. The list is a scroll like the stock exchange tickers of the past. Names and identifiers of the ones deemed unfit for continued loyalty. Lucas is on this list, was on it prior to quitting his job and leaving his subsidized home.

It wasn't a painful decision for Gail. He's made thousands of them, for all types of workers, even committing superiors he didn't trust. It's a special power, and those who have it are referred to as "deities." Gail's precision is considered uncanny, even among the deities. They know it's because of Rubal, the traitor grandfather who hardened his judgments. They are the only ones who know his age, his background, and his strange habits. The ones in D.C. reciprocate his loyalty by keeping him enigmatic. He may be one to rise to the upper levels, though there are so many vying for so few spots.

The Persian woman catches the last train west, squeezing through the dusk-lit crowd of beggars, her athletic arms twisting a path between hirsute citoyens who are dirty, relentless and vulgar. She shoves a limping hag away from the doors. Gail watches her lurch to a pole, find a handle, and then relax her face, neck and shoulders. It is like a warm breeze has passed through her. Her mouth curves almost into a smile. She touches her hair.

Gail has video of her in his home, scads of it. She has been inside hundreds of times, as she also accompanies the sanitation crews. Over time, she's changed her appearance in various ways. In some of the video, she looks like somebody else, only giving away who she is when she leans under his sink, places a hand on her hip, and checks the purifiers in her unique way. She tilts her head sharply, holds the test strips above her eyes, purses her brown lips, and counts the seconds by lifting fingers on her free hand. It is a routine she's unaware of and it caught Gail's attention early on.

He's never been there when she is. He always gets an alert when she's ten minutes away. His escapes typically include slipping out the back glass doors, over a retaining wall using an iron ladder, and into a walled garden that he shares with a Hidden man who avoids him out of fear. There is an urge for affection that Gail knows he has to resist. It will only do him harm. The tears that people shed, they are always the result of such affections.

Only once did he almost bump into her, coming out his front door when the alert failed to reach his button. He heard the murmur of her blocky truck, the whine of its worn out fan belts, and he stopped cold. It was a rare dry day, almost warm, and he paused to take off his suit jacket.

He saw the bleary orange light streaking along the glass walls around an empty curve. The grinding of her gears as she made the short climb up an embankment past the gate. Gail cut the other way, his shoes loud on the new cement. He sensed that she had come up the rise, parked with a thump in front of his building, just as he went out of view.

Now he watches the train rumble forward, staggering its passengers a bit. Some of the citoyens curse the riders and spit at the windows, while others laugh and point at the workers going home, away from the city. Gail touches the black glass with his fingertip like it's a pistol. He still sees the woman, her eyes closed now, her face mostly turned away as she engages in conversation with someone he cannot see clearly. As the train rolls out of view, she touches her neck lightly with her index finger.

He pulls out his button and pulls up her name and identifier. Her name, Anala, means "fiery" in Hindi. He highlights her and breaks her out of the list, drags her name into a file where she will be listed as "To Be Disappeared."

The man continues to come. Gail's doormat continues to get kicked around. Gail watches the video of him and is unimpressed. He is a boring man who frowns all the time and has a nervous tic whenever he walks past Gail's shelf of glass figurines. They are simple farm animals sculpted in a classic technique. The horses nuzzle the shelf under their hooves, as if feeding—they don't rear in battle mode or show any emotion; the shepherd dogs stand at attention and don't lie about lazily or cutely; and the bulls look absolutely bored, not defiant. The man's head jerks in short, hard snaps up and to the right every time he goes by them. This is the only thing about him that Gail finds interesting.

After the frowning man's latest delivery, Gail gets news of the missing Water Purification employee, Lucas. He was seen at a biology warehouse, stealing fish eggs. The intel says the eggs are used to grow fish for food. And this is not good. The outliers and citoyens need to be starved away, not fed. And how can any non-government water support a homemade fishery?

Gail wipes his face. He takes a minute to inspect his figurines. They are the only childhood items he has not destroyed. Other than these old figurines he has no letters, no photographs, no mementoes of any kind to remind him of the people, and the life they shared, on Rubal's farm.

They purify on-site, Gail types. Smart people. *I will talk to the Transportation friend. I expect to locate the runner, if the friend knows his whereabouts.*

The bigger issue is the lake, intensely polluted now, and whether it can remain as the water source for the nuclear plant. There is a lot of disagreement here, because testing is useless right now. The liquids are in a volatile state of flux, and the results run the spectrum from fair to toxic. Some are claiming it's already contaminated by the old cooling pools, essentially a radioactive bathtub that will catastrophically harm the core if used.

Others say it's safe to use, considering the alternative—to import a dry-cooling process—which would crumple the old reactor.

Lose/lose. No safe bet. Roll the dice. All are phrases that Gail is tired of hearing. And he is tired of relaying them to higher levels. There was chaos in the strategy, is what an old mentor used to say. The fellow would say it in regards to a failing system, often in the militaristic sense.

Gail feels it applies right now. It worries him deeply that science is at a loss. He can't afford to lose Lucas. There is nobody better at cutting through the wads of data. Despite his tendency to mourn dark numbers, Lucas always interprets them correctly. During these all-hands-on-deck modes, this is when you lose people. That was when Rubal veered off the path, having discovered intentional government-tainting of water and food. That was done to further separate the citoyens, already a dysfunctional lineage (a "new race" of malformed beings, as they were considered), from the rest.

Rubal said it was kicking a horse when it's down. He said it was even worse than that. He hollered and cursed, drank and fought with the farriers in the stables, coming inside bloody and torn at all hours during a volatile month when he went from unseen dignitary to spewing anarchist.

Rubal jumped ship. Gail cannot forgive him for that. The entire family nearly went to prison. Gail's little sister, then just a toddler of two, disappeared. It was bedlam, a hell brought to them by one man's principles.

Gail asks if there is any leeway to make an imperfect choice. They don't know. He asks if there's any time to delay using the lake, and they point back to the hazards of dry-cooling the spent rods. He's furious with everyone. He wants to know why they've been backed into such a corner.

He goes out on the restricted balcony at his office and looks at the low-running clouds, hears the lambent, approaching call of the train. He checks Anala's status on his button, finds her name in the crawl of text and numbers. *Outbound to Desert Camp*, a labor prison in the West. She'll likely live a life not too far removed from her Raleigh existence.

* * *

Sometime during the night, the intruder sneaks into the geodesic and lays a heavy dusting of lime on the water, dumping as much as he can stand while trying to breathe through the sleeve of his coat. When he's done he closes the door back and looks at it, unlocked, and considers the stupidity of humanity. He crawls through the mud between houses and huts, careful to keep his eyes from glittering in the glow from kitchen windows and weak security spotlights.

He growls at the dog Bixby, who watches him through the kitchen window, and the shepherd mutely bares its fangs but cannot leave the house. He rests against a spruce and gazes through the darkness at the forms of natty goats on the hillside across the river, above the church. They bleat into the wind and nobody hears them, so he takes one and slaughters it on the floor of an abandoned funeral home, where bodies had been gutted and repaired crudely for two centuries—before the waste began taking its toll.

In the parlor he finds a hearth where he roasts the goat, feeds moldy hymnals into the fire, and eats the meat in a ravenous fit, draining the commodes for water to wash it down with. When he is done, he opens a window and lets the air plow through, catch the flames, and engulf the dilapidated Victorian just before he has to run, his belly full, back into the wild wet darkness that is an endless amusement for people like him. He prefers the ruins and will turn his back, violently, on any kindness they offer.

10.

There was nothing wrong with the church when the last preacher arrived, nothing that he and a few able-bodied parishioners couldn't fix over the course of a warm and rain-free weekend. Back then, people were still comforted by experts who said the water and the air could rebound, if provided just a few years of proper, diligent maintenance. It was one of those things you could fix, like a worn-out freeway. This preacher, a young man with a fresh-faced wife and two giggling daughters, was the type who wore suspenders and cultivated a throwback air by combing his hair sharply to one side and maintaining a full beard.

They fixed leaky pipes and reseeded the lawn, patched wiring that had gone bad, and even installed new speakers in the steeple so they could "ring" the bells at noon daily, and just before services. It all came together nicely.

The preacher gave a lengthy sermon one Sunday, when there had been a two-week spell of steady mists and curious fish kills in the nearby lakes, about believing in hard things. He spoke about the miracles God performed to show Gideon … to prove to Gideon …

And the preacher scratched his head and smiled nervously and looked out to his flock. He opened his mouth and nothing else came out.

They had to take him upstairs to lie down. His wife told him that some rest would sort out his troubled mind. She said he had been through a sea of troubles with his family back in Kentucky and once he rested then he could return to the pulpit and preach as God intended.

So she finished his sermon, which was full of hopes to propel the people of Bynum to pray for a healed Earth, but to do so selflessly, being humble before God. They finished the service with a hymn and the good loving wife went upstairs to check on her weary husband (who had suffered such troubles with his family back in Kentucky) and found him dead in their bed, with black blood draining from his nose, eyes, and ears.

She was so distraught, so utterly shocked and dismayed by his sudden death, that she raised the bedroom window and leapt to her death. Their two giggling daughters were expedited to Kentucky, to live out their lives with the preacher's troubled family.

In a flash this story rose like smoke throughout the town and beyond, filling the corridors of suspicious minds with evidence that the world was indeed now a haven for evil spirits, that there would certainly be lachrymose endings for all angels, and doom and gloom for anyone who dared to hope otherwise. It was the origin of all ghost stories here.

It is not for Orel to know that these little giggling girls took their glow-in-the-dark letters and pasted them inside his closet wall just hours before they were rushed off to Kentucky. *Never let this darkness keep you.* He has no way of knowing, but would marvel at the fact that this lurid warning has glowed in his closet for nearly fifty years. It would seem impossible, perhaps even bedeviled. So it is best he does not know.

But he does know that the preacher was having terrible headaches in the days before his brain hemorrhage. There was a thin diary in the cabinet under the sink downstairs, in the tiny bathroom just off from the sanctuary. He figures it must have been overlooked all these years because it was propped against the back wall, flat, in virtual darkness. He only finds it because he is tasked with fixing all the problems with the indoor plumbing, as his father has taught him. He is down there with a drop light and a pipe wrench, about to set to work, when he sees the leather-bound journal with embossed letters.

He soon learns that the preacher is not so in love with his wife, that she became pregnant after only their third date. The preacher had been sleeping with one of his cousins in Kentucky and had borne a child with her, a boy with a physical disability who would die at the age of four. It is right after this loss that the preacher (who now has two school-age daughters) moves his family to North Carolina. But he is madly in love with his cousin and decides to start dampening his pain with alcohol.

There are pages upon pages of wild entries where the preacher is obviously out of his mind, so confused that he cannot write coherently about anything, not even the day of the week. There are others where he is surely strung out because the entries are terse and highly critical of God and anybody who believes in Him. Even food takes a beating.

Then there is the preacher's last entry, dated one soggy Sunday morning, where he declares it is time to turn over a new leaf and love his wife and daughters, and only his wife and daughters, as a husband and a father should.

Orel does not know of the preacher's sudden and tragic death upstairs. Nor does he know of the new widow's suicide on the heels of this tragedy. And he can never know of the giggling girls' weeping route to troubled family in Kentucky. Ghost stories are one thing; brutal deaths are another.

But he has seen the eerie letters and the words they spell out in his closet. He has an idea, a very good idea, that something went terribly wrong in this church.

* * *

Kione is out at first light, storming around in silence, trying to put the pieces together. There is a fire-gutted funeral home and a tank of dead smolt, and he is assuming both are the work of the same deranged soul.

"You know who did this," he hisses at Lucas, when the sleepy-eyed bioengineer answers the banging at his kitchen door. "And you are going to help me fix it."

They go to Kione's hut, which sits in a cluster of leaning structures high up the hillside above Gerard and Nan's home. It is not Spartan, as Lucas had expected. Kione is something of a packrat and the place is disorganized and cramped. He rakes a pile of laundry from a wood chair and points for Lucas to take a seat there.

A question-and-answer session ensues, with two brews of organic tea and lots of headshaking by the ex-mercenary, who listens intently to everything the bioengineer tells him. Lucas takes peeks around every time he is on the listening end, trying to gauge if Kione is insane or just way too busy in his role as protector to even put his dirty dishes in the sink.

"You've seen it," Kione says. "Not everybody here has. In fact, I'm not sure there's anybody here who has seen much in the way of brutality—like it is out there. There is a lawlessness like, what, not since the Middle Ages?"

Lucas shakes his head. "Bronze Age stuff," he says.

"Sounds right. It's pretty cruel and berserk all the time, everywhere. These people, like Gerard and Nan, I don't think they know ... not like you and me do."

Lucas nods. It looks like the refrigerator door is open and either the light is out or the appliance is not plugged in. He figures somebody else cooks for Kione. You couldn't prepare any worthwhile meals in here.

Kione keeps talking, explaining the tried-and-true method for smoking out and executing a lunatic. It is a harrowing game at times, but the payoff is thrilling, what the blonde soldier describes as an inexorable rush. He twists an imaginary skein of flesh in his hands, like you would wring out a dishcloth, and grins—practically leers—at the calm scientist, who is now his cohort in vengeance.

"What do you say?" Kione says, going back into his chair and lighting a cigarette. He smokes an endless army of cigarettes, wetting the spent burnt end of each as he deposits them in a jar filled with dirty water. "Do we have a deal?"

They shake hands like a couple of boys agreeing to a petty scheme, not the murder of a soulless arsonist and murderer. Lucas is not sure why he is involved, beyond Kione's hunch that this old citoyen is likely seeking some crude revenge on Orel for taking photographs of the murdered girl.

The boy's documentary of this vile event is already circulating the wires. It was an inhumane event, but it has shocked some of Orel's peers awake. It is helping to create a new mood among young people, and it has caught the eye of the ones who are sending broadcasts around the globe. One of the boards calls it a cry for a new moral fabric, a profound scene of "last hope," meant to strain, even shatter, the tone of morose surrender that prevails now.

Orel has told his father that students are not yet ready to bow out, that they see a future, even if their current leaders, parents and professors do not.

"Your generation gave up," Orel said. "Mine has not."

Outside of Kione's hut, a fog hangs over the hillside, dampens the soil so that it becomes a sludge Lucas has to slog through. He wipes his face with a cloth he found inside one of the dressers in the church, notices he has not shaved since arriving to this community. He grins, thinking he may become one of the long-beards before the end of spring, or at least summer.

Nan calls him as he passes their house. She has been trying to hang potted flowers around the porches, doing what she can to remind people it is springtime on an Earth that still has some variety of seasons, no matter how blurred the changes are now. There are peonies and begonias, a couple of mixes, and a bright weedy bowl of trillium that hangs right by the front door.

"I am so sorry to hear about your fish," she says, wiping her hands in a gardener's apron where she now keeps a pistol tucked in a front pocket. "They're all gone from what I hear."

"Every one. A total loss."

She shakes her head and tsk-tsks. Nan says there is no harm in planning another attempt, if that's what he has in mind. But she does not let Lucas answer. She keeps right on talking as she looks down on him through the fog.

"I've already got my boys in your geodesic cleaning out the tank. They ran off the water into an old cistern where Drake says we should put any bad water we come across. I hope that was the right thing to do. Anyway, we'll have that tank cleaned out by end of the week. Never say never around here, if you get my drift."

He isn't sure he does, but she disappears behind a slab of fog before he can gesture or say anything, and her voice keeps right on coming through it.

"Let me tell you a story, Lucas. It'll be worth your time, I guarantee it."

She emerges from the brume, hands on her hips like a politician or a Roman orator, heading full steam into her fable.

It is a righteous retelling of the events she witnessed in the Navy, right before she met Gerard and started having children.

She was on a cutter in the cold North Sea, sailing alongside the French and having a gloomy time of it, since they had been months out of port. There is a miasma, she tells him, which occupies a ship when it has been so long out to sea. A stench.

"Like a baby's rear end," she whispers, "when it has rash and diarrhea. Only worse."

This is when they came across what appeared to be a floating salmon ranch guarded by several small leaky Nordic boats.

"You can picture Vikings," she tells him. "It was a lot like coming across a few karves, all of 'em manned by fat dirty Finns who didn't like our coming so close to their operation."

There was a stalemate of a day or so, with the Finnish vessels growing antsy to leave and sail home because the crews were hungry and thirsty for alcohol. Nan isn't sure why her ship and the French ship kept sitting there at anchor. Nobody did anything wrong there. Perhaps the farm was a little too far into international waters, or maybe it wasn't.

"But orders are orders," she sighs.

So late into the second or maybe the third night of the standoff, Nan was standing watch on the starboard side, facing the floating ring of the fish farm, when there was a roar from the karves, a flare shot into the starry sky, and the sound of commotion in the water.

They threw lights from the cutter to the sorry Viking boats and saw that one of them was sinking, the one in the middle, and that its crew was leaping from the gunwales. While the American and French crews scrambled to their lifeboats, one of the other fishing boats started to sink, leading to even more panic and bedlam, just as the lifeboats hit the water and uniformed sailors were buckling their life vests. More flares were fired, causing the surface of the smooth black ocean to smoke, with coils of glowing vapor like a horror movie. The U.S. captain ordered his lifeboat crews to halt.

"You could tell something wasn't right," Nan says, narrowing her eyes. "A sinking boat is one thing. Two sinking boats is another thing altogether."

All the sailors stared silently at the fishing fleet, which was now just one boat rocking wildly as it is besieged with rescued Vikings. It was like a pack of dogs jumping onto a wobbly floating pier, only there were too many of them and this last seaworthy karve began to take on water just like the others. More flares were fired, including one that impaled a mast-climbing fisherman who dropped into the frothy sea like an ember.

"It was the craziest thing I ever saw," she says sadly, wiping her damp hair from her eyes as a new shroud of fog begins to crawl atop them. "Not a one was saved."

Lucas asks if they know what sank these fishing boats. It seems this is the mystery of it all.

"Somebody filed a report that said it was mischief, that it must have been the work of saboteurs."

"Do you agree? I mean, you kind of have to, right?"

Nan shrugs as she begins to vanish in the fog again.

"It's not what matters to me now. What matters, and here is where you are wrong, Lucas, is that we finally got to take a look into the ring. We went right up and stuck our nose into the water to see what kind of fish-ranchers these Vikings had been. And you know what? It was the second craziest thing I ever saw, for there wasn't a fin or a scale in that thing—not a fish to be found. Just water. Dark, cold, empty water."

"Strange."

"You're telling me."

"So what am I to take from this, Nan? What does your story mean to me?"

He can hear her but not see her. She is opening the screen door to go in and talks loudly back over her shoulder.

"Anybody can mess up, Mr. Lucas. We've all done it. But it's no good putting human lives on the line for something you can't see, for a purpose that you can't define."

"I'm still not getting it."

"Raise more fish, but let's kill that criminal before he kills us."

11.

Nico takes Orel to a downriver bluff, a clay monster that is almost impossible to climb up on. Orel gets nasty wounds on his hands, tears his flannel pants in the knees against jagged stones along the walls, and nearly plummets to his death when they hike too near the edge of a precipice above the roiling Haw below.

"I thought I'd lost my camera." Orel grins with embarrassment when they stop for lunch on the top, a muddy knob under a nest of dead beech trees. There are lazy vultures in the limbs of nearby snags, scouring the landscape for comestible death. Orel's lens glides silently in their direction, hones in on the scavengers, and he clicks several times before one of them glares down.

"This is a lost place," Nico says, handing a sandwich over. "Kids used to come up here and fly kites or fish with their parents, all kinds of things." He looks around and chews, makes a face. "But this is what it's good for now: vulture-spotting."

Orel nods. One of the vultures starts to preen and there is a loud piercing call far off somewhere, maybe a hawk. He squints at the birds through a fine mist. One of them drops onto a leafy shrub below.

"It's like the end of the world," Orel says. "A very damp and depressing apocalypse."

Here is where his new love disagrees. Nico says there is beauty here, plenty of it. And a lot of life—you just have to look for it. And that does not mean lifting up stones and finding snails or bugs, he adds.

"It's a waiting game," he says, tugging a thick cap on his head while Orel wraps his familiar leather scarf around his face, as though they are mujahedeen crouched in the rocks of the Pamir Mountains, waiting for word from Allah to descend. "You have time to meditate here, to counsel with beauty and nature."

"Are you a poet?" Orel asks.

"I'm not."

They gaze out over the desolate valley: a gray marsh that slithers between stony bluffs and chafed woodland banks, the dying wisp of a river on its weary path to the Atlantic Ocean. There is a nuke site downstream that wrecks the last miles of the waterway, a nuke that failed before their parents were born.

"My mother was a poet," Orel says as he stands and smacks clay from his pants. "She taught in the university and she wrote at home."

Nico says he has tried to read poetry but has never been able to fully understand it.

"Don't worry," Orel says, "my mom said nobody understands poetry, that you can only hope to be happy and at peace in its presence."

There is another sharp cry, this time closer, from a hawk. Nico fingers the pistol in his cargo pocket and tries to see if there is anything moving below. The only sound is the long hiss of the stream as it meanders through, and a sucking noise every once in a while from the vultures.

They use exposed roots to scale down the bluff and drop onto a pebbly beach below. Nico says they used to catch fish here, but not anymore. Orel takes a few pictures, and has to dry off his camera before returning it to his bag. They are going south along the flow, where maybe a half-mile farther down there is a gravesite for some of the people who lived here before. The government outlawed cemeteries decades ago and it is one of the few that hasn't been looted or bulldozed over. Nico says it used to sit back in the woods, draped in thickets, but only in recent months has it been exposed— mostly by an ice storm in early winter which shredded this part of the forest.

They march along, taking their time, with stops every so often to take out the camera and snap a couple shots. Just before they reach the cemetery, Nico pulls out his button and taps a reply to his mother.

"She isn't *worried* about us, she says," Nico groans. "Just *thinking* about us. I call that worrying, don't you?"

The cemetery is small, pushed up under a steep cliff that used to have a paved road tracing its spine. There are stumps all over, and cracked limbs and fragments of vines and twigs— so much woody waste that Orel wonders if a bomb didn't go off.

Some of the headstones are leaning, or pushed over altogether. There are a number of marble mausoleums, including a few that are in the throes of sinking. Crosses hang with the remnants of vines; a cherub turns its smooth face to the sky and spreads its palms wide in apologetic calm. Angels bow their heads, gallant fonts tell the names and give epitaphs and the birth and death dates of a dozen or so WHITLOW dead who appear to have come to America after the Civil War. Orel takes photographs.

There is a husband-and-wife tomb with no date of death for the wife, who would be nearly two-hundred-years-old by now.

"I wonder how she kept away from here?" Nico laughs.

A cat skeleton lies atop a grassy plot with a child's blocky headstone saying *Called By One Who Loves Him Dearly*. They take a few moments to debate whether this was the little boy's cat, or just a stray that wandered in and died. The boy has been dead a hundred years. With all these vultures, this cat is new by comparison, Nico decides.

"Let me get its picture," Orel says.

In the rear of the cemetery, where the cliff rises, they come to a vault that is stained black from years of steady moisture and dripping mud. They push at the massive door but it only creaks and will not pivot at all. There is only enough room for the camera lens to poke through; Orel slides it up and down the opening, steadily passing light through the shutter.

Then they look at each other and shrug, say it is time to go back and get out of the mist for a while. They return by the root ladder, the clearing under the vultures and their stark beeches, the muddy trails snaking up the hillside, and at last the broken concrete of the descent onto the bridge where lampposts have become roosts for the occasional great blue heron.

"I left my lens cap at the cemetery," Orel pouts as they stroll into the yard and see where Nan has hung flowers along the porch. "It's the last place I remember having it."

"That's fine," Nico says. "We'll go back and get it the next time we want to have our lunch among the tombs."

* * *

Gerard stands on the scaffolding beside the tank and brushes at the wall to scour whatever calcium oxide remains. Inside the steel circle, Eddie Drake alternately wipes with an old sheet and vacuums with a rumbling hose. He shakes his tufty head every time he thinks about it.

"You know what we used to call these types?" he hollers up to Gerard, whose face is red with work. "We used to call them 'bogeys.' You get a bogey, you take him out of circulation. Because he will only do harm to your cause and your loved ones. You snuff him like a damned worm."

Gerard laughs. He takes a break and watches the old-timer drag the hose around, unable to determine who is in charge: man or machine. Drake snarls on that it was bad enough to let Kione into the community because they'd never had any trouble from the outside anyway.

"I'm more of afraid of *him* than who is on the outside," the old man says lowly. "And now there is Dr. Lucas, and the son who is always taking pictures of everybody."

"He's not a doctor," Gerard corrects.

"Regardless," Drake says, puffing his cheeks as he nearly loses control of the wriggling hose. "This is yet another man who comes along with big ideas and even bigger troubles. One step forward, two steps back."

"I think you're jealous," Gerard teases, "because he knows more about fixing water than you do."

"I wish he did!" bellows Drake. "If he knew half of what he claims to know, we'd be in business. You can already see he doesn't know anything about fish farming."

Gerard says it's not Lucas who is to blame for the poisoning.

"Then whose fault is it? Mine? Yours? There's always a lot of blame to go around, but in this case all the blame points to our newest resident, Mr. Dr. Lucas."

Gerard keeps listening as the old farmer rants on, moving his own materials around now to test for lime residue like Lucas instructed him to do. From what he can tell, he and Drake have removed the last of it from the tank.

"You can step out now, Drake," Gerard announces, prying the particle mask from his face. "We're done."

Drake peers up and gives a look of mild disgust.

"Well what am I supposed to do, jump out like a Chinese acrobat? Lower that ladder in here so I can climb out, Gerard."

The door creaks open and Kione and Lucas walk in, looking like they have just finished a one-sided chat. Kione lights a cigarette and lifts his eyebrows.

"You and Hocus Pocus already cleaned it out?" he asks. Gerard points into the tank where the old man is trying to get himself onto the first rung of the ladder.

"Eddie's just coming out now," he says.

"Good." Kione turns to Lucas. "No reason not to start now, is there? I can give a hand if you like. Just tell me what to do."

"We need to go and get more smolt," Lucas says, his face somewhat pained. "You ... you might need to help me convince my friend that he owes me another favor."

"Done. Done and done. Are we taking your car or mine?"

* * *

Not far from the outskirts of the city on the south side, between a slew of railroad switches and snarls of rusty tracks, there's a cinderblock compound with painted-out windows and a series of iron vents fastened to its roof. Smoke billows from most of these vents, thick and white like you see from forest fires or bombs.

"Park us right here," Lucas says as they rattle up to a sliding metal door that has a series of Xs and *DO NOT ENTER* warnings spray-painted on it. Kione sets his parking brake and shoulders his rifle and they go to the door, where

Lucas presses a buzzer. It takes a couple of minutes before a voice scratches through the speaker over their heads.

Lucas negotiates their way in, seeming to know the gatekeeper well enough to not be nervous at all. Inside they quickly walk up one dark tunnel and then another before exiting into a large, low-ceilinged room with dozens of doors along its wide walls. Lucas takes them on a beeline for the door marked *SPACE: THE FINAL FRONTIER?*

The guy who answers is a stubby fellow with black-framed glasses who is sucking on a lollipop and wearing a white lab coat. His nametag says he is "Chuck F. Norris." He is not happy to see Lucas.

"They've put you on the list, amigo," the guy says, glancing nervously at Kione—whom he doesn't realize is on an even more egregious list: a kill list. "You know I can't help you, not anymore. They've put you on the list, man. And I can help a lot of chicos, but not somebody on that list."

He sees Kione's rifle and starts shaking his head.

"You gotta go, amigo," he says, putting his hands up to back them out of his doorway. Kione removes the rifle from his shoulder and lowers its hole at the guy's face.

"Just real quick help us out," he says in a soft voice, "and then we're gone."

Lucas looks around the room, walks back to where there are stainless-steel cabinets, side by side like they're waiting in line for a train. He goes to one in the middle, flings open the door and pulls out a fat jar filled with green-glittery fluid.

"Don't even need a crate this time," he says. "I'll just hold it in my lap."

Kione smiles a little. The guy has an earring fashioned like a boy shouting into a megaphone. It's from some cartoon that was popular when they were kids.

"Walk us to the door," Kione says as he pats the guy on his shoulder. "Don't be rude."

When they get outside Kione yanks the guy out with them and slams the butt of his rifle against the buzzer so that it shatters. He tells the guy to turn around and squat so that his face is against the metal door. As soon as the fat little guy works himself into position, they roar off and throw gravel and broken glass all over his back.

"These are exactly the same," Lucas says, holding the jar up and peering through once they are out of range of the city and off the freeway. "I don't know where he's getting them from, but these are remarkable in this day and age. Kind of a miracle, actually."

Kione lets the truck stay in neutral as they lean around a steep bend and wind down a hill that will eventually drop them right into Bynum. It is growing dark and the lights of the community are starting to sparkle through the empty trees.

"I remember miracles," Kione says. "They used to exist in the way-back days."

12.

The grandmother pries the plywood covering off of her one window, no bigger than a shoebox. She breaks two of her curly fingernails and sucks on what's left, like a child does. Carefully she stands on an ottoman already pushed to the wall there, raises her chin over the sill and gazes out—like a prisoner who has finally been given a view of the land beyond the walls.

What she sees are browned boards (a split-rail fence Gerard built for the livestock pen two years ago), stacks of new and old ceramic jugs that Nan uses for watering things and keeping feed grain dry, and several handled tools, such as the shovel Cyril used to bury the dogs. And then there are the dregs of the dying forest on the ground, leaves and husks and hollow limbs. A skinny rabbit sniffs at Nan's jugs.

She goes to her armoire and searches on her shelf for the pistol but it isn't there. Nico took it. He knew his father would not let him have one. But the old woman wants it now, because she is ready. It has been long enough and she is prepared, galvanized against doubt. But all she finds is dust and lace things, a few scraps of jewelry that she remembers another woman having, years ago, when the sun danced on the lake and people sang in auditoriums about important things like love and despair. She quietly drops it all to the floor just to make sure the shelf is empty. She rubs the smooth walnut and recalls that somebody used to polish nice things like furniture and dinnerware.

Then she goes back to the window and watches. Two pairs of legs wrapped in canvas from the knees down go by, short legs, like they belong to boys. One of them runs and she puts her hands over her ears because these boys are always shouting. They are usually accompanied by barking dogs. She wonders where the barking has gone off to, if something has happened to the dogs. She remembers a boy crying not long ago, maybe thirty years.

And then the fat woman who married her son is yelling about the intruder. The *intruder*. The woman is afraid again and she knew she had to be ready if it ever came to this again. She promised herself it would never happen again, *never*. Not never, not ever, ever, ever, never. But she knew it would.

Like the wind blows, her husband used to say. *Like the wind blows, my darling. Over and over again, because it has no beginning and it has no end.* Something like a song he used to sing. And he sang when he was happy, never when he was sad. Rarely was he sad. Only when he was little. He reminded her that it was a waste of time to be sad, that you could only get things done if you were happy.

Joyous! That's a ridiculous word. And now that the legs are gone, there is nothing. The wet earth stinks even through the walls of her room. The skinny rabbit hiding between the jugs, peeping out once the boys have left. It has eyes dark like berries. It used to be afraid of the dogs. Maybe this is the intruder. A scrawny hare? They used to raise rabbits when the lake sparkled and they sang Mozart in the opera houses downtown. The rabbits were twitchy things with eyes like blackberries. Skin them and hang the meat in the trees.

The grandmother steps down from the window and draws down a rope from the beam where Gerard often hangs a decoration, for Christmas or her birthday. It is easy to pull enough of it down and leave the rest of it up there. She takes a little time to scooch the ottoman over. It must be full of stones or bones or something people don't like to get rid of but want to hide from the others. Like that pistol! Or whatever a rabbit hides in its hole. Maybe it is sheet music and they are going to take it out and sing from it when she is gone. Singing for weeks on end. She loosens the end and smiles to think that her pretty head has something in common with the decorations that her son puts in her room like this. She smiles and pretends she is a string of mirthful shiny things and is going to take a walk …

* * *

The peaceniks light night fires at the slags now, to have a light roaring in the abyss, hoping this will keep the intruder away. Fire has no eyes, it cannot see, so the intruder is not afraid of it. He is not sure what they plan to achieve by using it. Did they not see the state he left the funeral home in? Surely they can't think he is intimidated by fire. It must be for their own purpose that they burn these pyres in the darkness.

He slithers through a cleft in the tomb and rests his head on a pile of straw. He peels the dead skin from the back of his hand—not always do you escape fire without injury—and slings it against the wall, where it smacks and sticks. He eats a rabbit that he roasted on one of their fires. He even chews the crooked leg bones and swallows the boiled fluids inside its guts.

He laughs. When he was a boy, his mother said he laughed like a thunderstorm. So he closes his eyes whenever he laughs and imagines jags of lightning, glossy urban dreamscapes in black ice and endless night scarred by his ravaging crimes, whole blocks of apartments oozing rainwater, soiled by blood and carnage. He wants the end of the world, and he wants to be a part of it. His mother rolled her eyes back in her head when she injected and sighed about her baneful son, calling him *liebe vogel*, her lovebird.

The intruder sweats in the crypt as he sleeps, knocking his knees against the bones and shoes of the dead. He knows they have been here because they left prints, like starving nomads who travel in circles wherever they go. There is also the lens cap with *CANON* on it, and he remembers the one boy with the buzz cut staring through the window.

It's about to be light and the intruder is sore from a day of cutting his way through underbrush and the fall he took coming down a bluff as he pursued a goat. He knows they have guns and he wants one. A gun would change everything. With a gun he could slaughter the timid and the wicked alike, and not have to wait for the unwary to wander into one of his traps.

His mother used to gloat over his prowess. She would tell her junkie friends he was vile, yes, but merciless with strength and cunning, like some beast unleashed from hell itself. She swore that his father had given an oath to her that her son was some new type of being, an ultra-human. The father claimed the government had spiked his seed with a genetic cocktail.

But the intruder is getting old now, and he reckons himself to be more than seventy, but not yet eighty. His limbs are growing heavy and his joints are drying out, but he knows he is stronger and more durable than most. He believes his father and has lived his life accordingly. He knows there is enough lore spread through the citoyens for a man to have a legacy, even if it is depraved, and can only be spoken among the adults. He wants to be one of those whom they speak about. But more importantly, he wants to kill these people in these huts and domes, because they have enough food and water for him to live out his remaining days here, solitary and triumphant.

* * *

Lucas is once again awakened by blows against his kitchen door. It is daylight, barely, and here is Nan. Her face is streaked with sooty tears, babbling about another death, a suicide this time, and how her dear large-nosed husband may also be to the end of his rope.

"I well expected to find her dead one morning," Nan says as he pours her coffee at the table, "but not like this. She was stiff as a rod. I hadn't been down there since yesterday. Some days I give her the space she needs."

Lucas glances at his clock and sees it is six-thirty. There is a station of the cross for every hour and he is exactly between Veronica wiping Jesus' face and the good Lord's second fall to the streets of Jerusalem.

"Gerard is having her funeral tonight," she says, her voice catching in her throat. "He wants you to come. And bring Orel, please."

As the afternoon fades, they gather around Gerard's house, the biggest one in the community, and help set up tables and chairs on the porch. It starts to rain and the boys are draping tarps atop sturdy trees and posts they forced into the ground earlier. Somebody scatters a little dry pine straw under a tent that Gerard has designated *for music only.*

They carry out the grandmother's bier and set it atop benches down on the far end of the porch, where one of the men starts to fasten old iron wheels to it. Then they rest her coffin down on it and shroud her in a stack of her antique laces and thin quilts. Gerard sobs in Nan's arms.

"Let's get to drinking," Eddie Drake says as little Cyril and Torrey pick up their dulcimers and start playing. A couple or two start to dance sad waltzes on the porch.

Gerard ambles into the tent and stands between his younger sons. He starts to warble a rendition of an old song that turns all heads his way.

There are now a half-dozen men and women under the tent, gliding bows along the strings of fiddles, and blowing harmonicas, with quiet Kione setting up in the rear with a beautiful vintage hollow-body guitar that he's plugged into a small amp. They all dip into a version of "Lonesome Road Blues," and Drake takes a whiskey bottle and turns it upside-down so that it pours out the sides of his mouth. With his cheeks nearly bursting, he sprays the lode over a nearby barrel fire and hollers as the flame ignites.

"Do you mind?" Nan grins as she pinches Lucas's hand for a dance to a two-step that someone is guiding the band into. She is surprisingly light on her feet and adept at alternating between positions, from sweetheart to shadow to wrap. She kisses him on the cheek when they're done.

Up on the porch, a sallow woman is perched on the edge of a metal folding chair, all by herself. Lucas hasn't seen her before. He assumes by her complexion that she may be sick. But he has had all the vaccinations, so he sits down beside her anyway. She gives him a weary look.

"We don't mourn for the dead so much anymore, do we?" she drawls in a voice that is both feathery and heavy, as though two people are composing it for her. She wears a locket around her neck like people did before.

"There's no shortage of mourning," he replies. "Here, or anywhere."

The woman, it is hard to tell how old or young she is, is not convinced. She chews on her lip and gazes down at the pall where the grandmother lays in silence.

"There's most certainly a shortage of it here," she mutters, twisting her feet nervously.

The songs are broken by a meal that was prepared by some of the men and their wives, a roast goat with chestnuts and pears. The pears are canned from last fall, one of the men explains, though nobody listens because they are too busy loading their plates. They scatter along the porch (careful not to get too close to the departed) and sit, platters in their laps and drinks on the floorboards, eating and swallowing during the first silence in a couple hours. Nan comes by and takes the plates and glasses when they are finished. She apologizes that there is no cake or pie for dessert.

"Hell!" Eddie Drake hollers. "Let's start to drinking again!"

Deep into the night they go, some of them getting too drunk and either passing out or vomiting in the ditch behind the house. Nico and Orel take turns walking the drunkards home. Nobody is allowed to go around in the dark alone, and Nico has his pistol.

The wake is winding down as the clouds part a bit and let shine a few hazy stars. Nico is directing Orel as to where some of the constellations are, and Nan is convincing the younger boys to go ahead and crawl into their beds. Lucas stands by the barrel to warm his hands when the cheerless woman from the porch gently pokes him in the ribs. Her shoulders hunch a little even when she stands, though he can tell—especially in the shadows from the fire—that she is fairly young.

"You, for one, seem sad inside," she says softly as she pulls her cardigan down tightly over her shoulders. "You seem like you have a lot in your heart, but it has a hard time all getting out."

He smiles, making sure it is a big smile. The liquor in his belly is warm and it has—despite its tragic origins—been a festive day for him. And he has enjoyed watching Orel appear happy for the first time in years. Lucas tilts his head and believes there may even be a twinkle in his eye as he stares at the frail young woman. Despite her sickly complexion, she is pretty, the kind of pretty where a man just wants to touch her hair and sigh.

Lucas opens his mouth, his eyes locked into hers (anodyne, vast and dark), and his mind stifles. He puts a finger to his cheek and stares at her, unable to say anything, until finally she drops her eyes and walks slowly into the next group being chaperoned home.

13.

There is a bird on the cement railing as Lucas comes onto the bridge. He is one of the last to leave the wake and is sobering up as dawn approaches. The bird is a tall black silhouette on the parapet, shrouded within its own bleakness.

He kicks a rock that makes it only a few feet before it skitters into a pile of rubble and chinks against what sounds like glass. The bird swivels its narrow head and casts its glowing eyes on him, much in the way a cop or prison guard would do. Lucas is tempted, even from a distance, to touch his brow in salute.

But as he gets closer, he sees the bird has limbs, human legs, that drape over the side of the bridge, and that thick muddy boots are swaying—almost playfully—over the water. The "wings" are nothing more than arms wrapped in a sort of burial shroud or cloak, like would be used to inter a preacher. The eyes shine silver and the rabid intruder is behind them.

Lucas does not have a gun. He left it at Gerard's, and the man on the bridge sees him patting empty pockets and leers as he swings his legs back over onto the span. Only a few yards separate them, and the intruder draws an ugly sword from his garments and brandishes it menacingly.

"Wait," Lucas stutters as he holds up his hands and drifts back, in the middle of the road, until he is stopped by debris. "Wait," he says again. He wonders what use it would be to yell, if there is anyone awake and sober enough to help. Or even close enough to them. Orel left the wake a couple hours ago and is probably asleep. Even if he isn't, the church is a hundred yards off. Too far to hear.

"Come on," Lucas babbles, glancing around for something to put in his hands. The intruder advances deliberately, the sword flashing in the light from the flickering fires at Gerard's. Lucas has a tiny harmonica in his pocket that somebody thrust at him, drunkenly, on the promise that he would learn how to play it. He also has his keys. No matter what happens, the lunatic cannot get his hands on these keys. Lucas decides he will have to throw them in the river below if something bad starts to happen.

Lucas stoops to grab a chunk of cement-molded rebar, and the intruder comes at him in a rush, the blade glinting as he swings it for the skull. The sword clanks upon the steel that Lucas holds between his hands, and his opponent exhales wildly, having used so much force for the blow. They stagger in opposite directions and the intruder drags the tip of his weapon on the bridge so that it scrapes garishly. Then he wields it high over his head and lunges for his prey, his eyes luminous with obscene passion, spit flicking from his lips, and crashes it once more against the bridge fragment, throwing sparks this time.

The intruder howls into the end of the night and begins to pant like an animal as he draws more energy, stretches the cables in his neck, and bares his teeth for combat. He has paused only for a flash, a millisecond, and Lucas has flung the crude shield at his head, striking the wild man right in the temple. The intruder drops in stages, grunting and growling, first to one knee and then to all fours, before collapsing on the ground with a gust of breath.

Lucas stumbles over him and snatches the sword away before falling against the rail in a heap, his lungs convulsing. He tries to call out but cannot. He tries to move but he is paralyzed. He's not even sure that he's able to see, as there is so much darkness. All he can do is hear the sloshing river below, the Haw, smoothing its folds between mossy stones, heading southeast to the ocean in a continuous but unhurried coil.

* * *

They are slow to decipher what it means, this frightening pole stabbed into the ground—by some lunatic—in their village. Even knowing that the intruder is dead, they are baffled. Whoever raised this totem, and stuck it with bones and flesh from the dead, wanted to frighten them. And it worked, because even Kione is shaken.

Orel, his face pale, silently paces around the lurid marker and takes photographs. Every once in a while someone will point and murmur, lift their eyes around the pole, and Orel will go over and shoot a couple of frames for them. Everybody is taking away something different.

"It's just a sick man's idea of torture," Nico says through his teeth, knowing that the intruder dug up his brother's dogs and dissected their corpses, just for this. There is fur and teeth all over the things, not to mention the human relics used by this disturbed artist. "We should put parts of *him* on it," seethes Nico.

Kione and others quash this idea. After a brief inspection of his body, they set it on fire right where it lays on the bridge. Orel gets more pictures of this—including identifying photos of the deceased, in case anyone ever comes around looking for answers.

"We all know that this totem could help with our reputation," Kione says as he and Lucas have sandwiches inside the geodesic, beside the fish tank. "We have to leave it up, right? It's so bizarre, so *out there*—it could help protect us, make us seem that much more profane."

Lucas thinks about it, then nods. His view is that you cannot do enough to deter intruders, especially these ever-crazier citoyens. The totem is a complement to the community's reputation. It adds to the village's chilling mythology.

"It's like the castle at Disneyland," he tells Kione.

"What?"

They dump buckets of fish food into the tank, using a recipe from Eddie Drake. "Don't screw it up and put the stuff out of order," Drake growled at them as he handed over his worn notebook. It seems to be working well. The Coho are already the size of a child's hand, and they grow larger by the day.

"We should have turned that body into fishmeal," Kione says later, as they are locking up.

"We did," Lucas says. "Me and Gerard went out there while people were gathering fuels for the pyre. We cut off his legs and hands and some other stuff. I'm going to make a separate batch of Drake's food recipe and see how it works. My thinking is, it should work just fine. All I do is replace protein with protein."

Kione nods and gives Lucas a look from the corners of his eyes. Lucas doesn't seem rattled by the kill-or-be-killed encounter. The ex-soldier is pleased to see that the father is capable of protecting his son against full-on evil and aggression.

"You're coming along fine, Lucas," Kione says.

* * *

Lucas and Orel sit in the church and look up at the altar, the brass crucifix with the expiring messiah, the raised dais where robed choirs offered canticles for their God, and later themselves, as the world stumbled into gray decline. Lucas scans the stained-glass windows on the north side, his right, while his son observes the arched fenestration on his side.

The pews are all intact, screwed to the oak floors with rusty—but firm—anchor bolts. There are even some bibles in the racks behind the seats, gold-edged and thumbed through so that the pages flap in wobbly ways when Lucas pries one open. He has turned randomly to Leviticus and the chapters on uncleanliness, purity, atonement and holiness.

Orel is rubbing his palms together as he looks at one phalanx of windows, then the other.

"They're so dark ... like there's so much green that it overwhelms," he says finally. "I mean, you look at all the red velvet carpet and cushions ... and then all this green that washes in from this glass."

Lucas rubs his chin. There are leafy greens all over the glass depictions, from cedars to palms to the distant hills of Jerusalem, so much green. But he reminds his son that these windows were designed for the era before, when sunlight was prominent and the other colors—the golds and reds and blues—would capture the rays and shine them down into the sanctuary.

"This green is taking advantage of our—let's call it sadness. There used to be plenty of daylight shining through these walls I bet. They have spruces and firs planted around the church that would let ample light through. You see what I'm talking about, Orel?"

The boy frowns a bit but still acknowledges. All he has ever known is gray above, which is not the same as his father. Lucas has flickering memories of milky blue sky and maybe some sun, beyond the fleeing patches they get now. There used to be days of it, even weeks. It used to be strong enough to even burn off the fog and mists.

"I suppose," Orel sighs. He looks at his father, who has the black leather book in his hands. "What's that?"

Lucas looks down and flips the pages some more.

"It's your Holy Bible, hot off the presses," he answers, laughing softly. There was once talk of banning religion, and then religious conclaves put together a plan to ban governments. Both sides backed down eventually.

"Oh," Orel groans. "Never mind."

They scour the hall closets for amusements and find a trove of stuff, including ornate candelabras that could hold fat Christmas candles, vestments for baptisms and funerals, even a few staffs, which Lucas wonders about. They light a few candles, place them on the thick marble altar and continue exploring, heading now for the tiny chamber off to one side of the apse, a low door much like a pet entry. Lucas uses a hammer to break off its lock and pries his way in, immediately blowing at a nest of cobwebs.

"A forsaken place," he says in a comically low voice. He twists a flashlight beam inside and they are disappointed. Nothing but a handful of mobile kneelers and a stack of cheap, plastic collection plates. Lucas jokingly shakes one of the plates to make sure it is empty. He complains about the lack of authentic, weird things in the church. Not even a bottle of holy water.

They go into the kitchen and make a lunch. They drink coffee while they wait for the potatoes to boil. Lucas uses the moment to wind his wristwatch. He discovers the glass face is cracked, probably a result of the violent brawl with the intruder. He holds it to his ear and it still ticks fine.

Orel slides out of his chair and checks on the toast in the oven. They are using some of Nan's artisan pumpkin bread, which will soon be slathered with goat milk butter. Lucas clears his throat.

"I had a friend once, a history guy who graduated from Yale. He was a friend of your mother's and I met him through her. He was a real nice guy and read the best books, knew how to talk about painting and theater, and he kept himself busy writing papers on civilizations in the Middle Ages."

Lucas looks down at his coffee, from habit. You wait too long to check on it and a bug gets in, was the rule in the city.

"This guy, Raphael was his name, Raphael something—he went to Europe to study for a couple of years. Right about the time when you were born and we were all reaching thirty. Raphael went over to do research for a book the government was paying him to write—a huge book, both in size and scope. Raphael was kind of a genius."

Orel opens the heavy oven door and lifts the sheet of toasted bread out. He finds a wide knife and starts spreading the butter.

"He wrote us from time to time, called once in a while when he could. He traveled the whole time. There was a lot to see, a thousand libraries to forage through. He got sick in Turkey, or maybe it was Greece, and spent a whole month in the hospital. But he kept writing, and reading. Called your mother once to tell her about the helva—a dessert—he had one night. Sat in this hospital's cozy chapel with all these Turkish scholars, smoking cigars. Raphael was unique. He had charm."

Orel scoops the potatoes from the pot and begins seasoning them.

"He flew in to the city terminal, and your mother and I picked him up at his gate. He'd lost a lot of weight, shaved his head, and had grown a long curly beard, like Zeus or somebody. He still smiled, but it was a dim smile. His eyes didn't light up like they used to. His hands trembled a little bit."

Orel brings their plates to the table.

"Your mother said maybe it was the illness—he had a pretty bad case of typhoid. But I've seen people after they've had fevers like that and such, and Raphael wasn't down because he'd had typhoid. It was something else, something deeper than that. So he moved back into his apartment in the city, in this gray brick tower mostly occupied by Hidden, and he apparently dove into writing his book. We went three, four months without hearing from him."

Lucas waves his spoon at Orel and nods approval. The potatoes are delicious.

"We got a fat envelope in the mail one day and it was the first draft of his manuscript. He taped a note to it saying he would have sent it via the wires, but they weren't secure enough. The post is so corrupted, he said, nobody would imagine you would let them handle a sensitive document like this. And we sat on the couch a few nights, reading. Your mother spent a lot of her time with you then, since you were born while Raphael was overseas, and I was always nervous at work—the lakes all around had just suffered their first toxic algae blooms. It was a bad time with that.

"We read it all in maybe three nights, all six-hundred pages. Cover to cover, so to speak. And your mother was very quiet about it. She was usually verbose about things like this, you see. Your mother was a great teacher because she had a wonderful way of articulating her worries, her desires, her deepest and darkest cravings—she was collected, solid. You never had to worry if you were getting the whole story from her."

Orel collects the plates and lays them in the sink and runs warm water over them. He uses a mesh cloth to scrub them and then stands the dishes on a wire drying rack after rinsing. He starts to brew more coffee, using some Vietnamese beans Nan has sent over.

"Sila wouldn't discuss Raphael's manuscript. She said she couldn't tell me why. I'd read it, you see. I can't for the life of me figure out what was so alarming to her. It wasn't his usual brilliant stuff, not his best work by any means. But it was just a first draft. I assumed he'd punch it up as he went along. The framework was there and the facts were supported by research. Scientifically, it was a good history book."

Orel brings more coffee to the table.

"So, do you know what happens? Of course you don't, you were little. Well, Raphael went another couple of months working on a rewrite or whatever. We didn't hear a thing from him. Our life went on. The lakes took a nosedive, the borders collapsed, and then they walled them up. The government warped into the tight ventricle it is now, and your mother said she was going crazy. She wondered if we had done the right thing by bringing a child into this world. She got depressed and took a leave from her job. She never went back to work. And we waited for Raphael to send us the next draft, to call us and say come to the city and have dinner with him, or just stop by and catch up. But we never heard from him again. I saw a write-up in the paper one Sunday, a short article about people the government had rounded up for being subversives. Raphael was one of them."

"Was he the type?" Orel asks.

Lucas shakes his head and blows on his coffee.

"No more than I am," he says.

14.

Even if the skies seem frozen in a winter mode, Nan's calendar says the seasons are changing. And she's taking action to dispel the gloom that has set in to the village.

"It's spring!" Nan announces as she swings open the door to her guests. "Welcome to the feast! We have a feast for you two, and we want to hear you sing tonight. No ifs or buts."

Indeed, Nan has dressed up her dining room in pagan glory, festooning the beamed ceiling with every type of flower she could find in the woods, even creating a tiny rock waterfall in the center of the table.

"That's champagne," she beams as Orel pokes his finger into the stream curiously. "Cheap champagne, but it's still the old bubbly just the same. I just can't drink too much or it'll give me a headache."

She's making a headache face at him when Gerard comes in smiling, already clutching his guitar to his body in the ready position.

"Have you been practicing?" he asks the fledgling harmonica player, Lucas. "I'm going to be disappointed if you haven't."

Orel puts his hands to his head and flutters his eyelids.

"Believe me," he tells Gerard, "Dad has been *practicing* a lot."

They gather around Nan's enormous English leaf dining table, scrounging up chairs to fit everyone in. Cyril is chosen to serve what won't fit on the table and Nico fills glasses with water, promising that champagne is soon to come.

"I haven't figured out how to get glasses under the fountain without spilling it," he admits.

"Oh, son, it's like this," Gerard announces, thrusting his flute under the shimmering cascade until it brims, sloshing over a bit. "Or close enough," he adds with a snort.

They devour the brisket (don't ask how she got it, Nan commands) and are down to the wings on the duck before the hostess demands they slow down in order to leave room for dessert.

"I have pie this time," she smiles daintily. "And cake."

After dessert, they move to the parlor and the instruments are grabbed up. Torrey sits under the keys of an organ that sounds flat at first, but livens to an almost rockabilly fervor as his brothers join in on banjo and mandolin. They play an instrumental stomp that sends Nan into a skirt-swirling fit, her cheeks red as ketchup by the time the last bar fades.

"Bravo!" Gerard thunders, clapping wildly. "Hell yeah!"

In due time they are all swooning within the melody of a long-ago spiritual, its lilting harmony brushed to almost unbearable tenderness by the youngest boys' unchained vocals.

The champagne is all gone and they are sipping at strong Polish vodka, something that is easy to make around here, since Gerard's Irish ancestors, ironically, were once fervent gorzalka distillers. Nan's potatoes produce a staunch, somewhat pink-hued, vodka.

Gerard lifts his glass and offers a toast.

"To Orel!" he cries. "For getting accepted into Princeton!"

Everybody shouts huzzah. Everybody except Lucas, who had no idea. He searches their faces, still holding his full shot of vodka in the air.

"What?" he says.

Orel hurriedly explains that he just got word on his button the day before, right after they went scrounging through the church. It was after lunch or maybe before, he can't remember.

"I wanted to surprise you, Dad."

"You did."

"I wanted you to be happy about it."

"I am."

Gerard clears his throat and steps into the center of the rug, almost stepping on Bixby.

"He was afraid you would cry, Lucas," he offers gently. "He's afraid that you will be lonely without him. We told him you'll have us, so why not tell you in front of us."

"Really, it was my idea," Nan says, sounding serious for the first time all evening. "I'll make anything a good reason to put out a big fancy spread. And I knew he was nervous about telling you."

Lucas smiles and throws back his shot. "Huzzah," he says mildly.

Orel bows his head and twists his shoes into the rug. He is not convinced his father is excited about the news. Cyril punches him in the shoulder and says, "Cheer up, college boy."

Nan snaps her fingers and hoots.

"One last song!" she cries.

They gather up the instruments again, everybody switching around like they do, and Gerard melts his way into a bluesy paean to the rites of passage. Nan winks at Lucas, who is forced to thrum along on a dobro that he can only crudely manipulate.

Gerard, eyes shut tight and head tilted back, croons the end of the last verse. Then everybody thrashes through the final chorus, causing Bixby to bark and trot between their legs. Torrey laughs and reaches down to scruff the dog's ears, but is thrown into the chair behind him, his mandolin cracking into the wall. A dark jagged streak climbs up the plaster and disappears into the crown molding. The champagne waterfall lurches on the table and crashes apart, flooding the cloths and forks left behind. Bixby howls in terror.

"What the hell is happening, Gerard!" Nan shrieks, clutching at Cyril who was next to her but now stumbles around like his boots have become roller skates.

One of the windows in the kitchen bursts, showering the floor with glass. The hearth belches a smoky cloud of ash into the room and the lights flicker off and on again, causing a radio to roar in the corner—a woman's silky voice invoking her lost lover to return.

Then it stops. There is a hiss, but Gerard—his voice trembling—says it is not the gas. They all turn and look at the far window together, which faces south. It glows a ghostly yellow, like a pulsing sun is there.

"The nuke," Lucas whispers hoarsely. "They've gone and blown it up. It's melting down. You see it?"

Nobody says anything, they are so transfixed upon the lambent glass. Torrey is bleeding above his eye but doesn't say a word and nobody notices. They watch the distant nuclear reactor overheat, slowly shine white with blooming intensity, and then hold its blinding glare, accompanied by a tiny sound much like a child howling into a cave.

15.

When river water boils, it's certain that things are bad. It bleaches stone, scalds sediment and scorches lily pads and pickerelweed, laying waste to this already-perishing ecosystem. The catastrophic damage from the nuke remains close to its fluted reactor, but the fallout spreads like a disease, rapidly. The lake vanishes within hours, jettisoned into steam and vapors, and it dissolves into the roiling clouds above.

Forests lurch and burst into flames, leaving cinders to pock the earth and coil smoke in dense screens that delays rescue for thousands of citoyens huddled on the banks of nearby streams and creeks. They moan in desperation and begin the long cycle of starving to death. The clay earthworks guarding border towns and villages turn liquid, so that wild young take to them on canoes in doomed efforts to escape. The gases choke and strangle countless mothers clutching their children.

From the vantage point the peaceniks have, the worst of it is roughly forty miles southeast. There isn't much knowledge regarding the survival of a nuclear meltdown. It is the type of information that has been cast aside for several generations, leaving people to assume that such a disaster is inherently fatal. Nobody has plans for surviving something like this. There are no stocked cellars or doomsday dungeons, no rations hoarded in public warehouses for distribution.

Everybody is on their own.

The first night is horrific, as the glow downriver dissipates rapidly once it has done its cataclysmic harm. There is a sharp wind, like a storm gale, that follows behind the darkness. It lasts for several minutes, then subsides, leaving behind an eerie calm. They have all gone into the cellar, which Gerard will later say was a matter of instinct (like bugs darting for the corners of a room when the light unexpectedly comes on) and the need for a bit of quiet to gather his thoughts.

They stare at one another mutely. The image of the old woman swinging from the end of her rope, just a few short steps away, remains fresh in some of their minds. The rope itself is still wound around the beam, the widow's shoes still neatly placed beside her bed.

"I can't take it in here," Nan protests, clutching the top of her chest, her bosom heaving. "I have to go back up."

She clambers up the stairs and, with an apologetic glance behind, Bixby follows. The men and boys look around at one another. The lights dim and then rekindle. Gerard says he is going to scrounge around for candles.

"Let's just go back up," Lucas says, already taking steps toward the exit at the far corner of the room. Gerard follows the pack, muttering to himself. Upstairs, the wind has stopped howling. They can hear Nan rummaging in the kitchen. She is making coffee and searching for sturdy plastic or paper to put over the shattered window. Nico goes in to sweep up the glass.

The rest fall into chairs in the parlor where they were just singing and dancing. It does not feel like the same room. Bixby acts unsettled, fidgeting from one pair of feet to the next. Gerard reaches over to the radio on the table next to him and taps it, knowing it was just on during the blast. A timid male voice echoes out, asking vague questions of an audience that can't reply. He asks if anyone knows how to get in touch with God, because he seems to have lost Heaven's number.

Outside, the air thickens with returning fog, a miasma that wraps around trees and houses, a cooling mist that reclaims its place along the Haw. Lucas peers out the window but can see almost nothing. But there are dead birds on the bridge, and a frothy wave is heading down the river, and all the fires have been snuffed by the winds. The air smells of sweet sulfur, almost like garlic.

Lucas and Orel go outside while the others stay indoors to drink their coffee and listen to the radio for any updates. Their tablets have no connection and all the buttons are dead. Lucas wants to check on the others.

"The footing is poor," Lucas cautions as they maneuver down the hillside, eyeing the huts below where all is lit up like Christmas. Every light is on in every dwelling. Lucas pops open the door to the geodesic with the salmon tank, hears the purring pumps and breathes a sigh. He quickly locks it back and they move on, coming to Drake's place first.

Eddie is in thermal underwear and a flannel hat, smoking a cigar. His eyes are weary, bloodshot, and his movements are slow and almost too calm. He waves them in and sits them on an antique loveseat that he immediately starts talking about.

"My grandmother got it from France," he says, going into the kitchen to fetch drinks for his guests. "One of the last of its kind. Not so much comfortable as it is nice to look at, wouldn't you agree?"

The old man passes a paper cup of rice wine to Lucas.

"Sake's all I got," he apologizes as he sinks into his padded armchair. "So what can I do you for?"

Lucas blinks. He turns to his son, but Drake laughs.

"I'm sorry," the old man says. "I get a weird sense of humor when things get this bad."

Lucas comes forward, elbows on his knees, and starts describing what he knows of meltdowns. The ratio of contamination is going to be drastic or complete in some areas. All these years of keeping purified water, it's gone now. Zeroed out by radon. There won't be an animal worth eating for miles around. And that includes goat, poultry, fish, and reptiles.

"I think our salmon will be okay," he tells Drake, making sure this point gets across. "This is a steel tank, six feet of oxidized water. Should be good to go. But there's one drawback to this."

Drake looks up from his sake, unplugs the smoldering corona from his gob.

"It'll be the only food fit to eat for a hundred miles," he says, tapping ashes into a can at his feet.

Lucas touches his nose and nods.

"I sure hope it's a secret," he says.

Drake assures them it is, saying the only other person who might know is Lucas's buddy from the bio lab in the city. He asks Lucas if his buddy ever got any hint as to where these fish were headed. Lucas has to tap his lips and think about it. There may have been something said ...

"It's a long shot that he would even care," adds Drake, looking suddenly at Orel, who is making sure his camera still works. "Take my picture, sport," the old man chuckles, jabbing the stogie back between his yellow teeth. "The last of a breed."

They say goodnight to Drake and move down to the gloomy woman, the one Lucas chatted with at the wake. She is in low spirits. They are surprised to find that she keeps snakes in her hut, pets that she feeds mice and voles found in the reeds by the tidal eddies between landlocked boulders. She explains that this site, what she calls "the vortex," is formerly where town folk used to launder their clothes, nearly two centuries before.

The woman turns her eyes away and may be looking at somebody or something they can't see. Her expression becomes that of someone who is gazing at a lover, her mouth anxious for another's.

"I came here to get away from the madness," she says, her voice hushed yet still a mix of softness and grit. "I came all the way from Chicago, where it was much worse. It was so awful that I promised never to think of it again."

Lucas is rubbing his hands together, studying his shoes. Orel is on his own and will have to fend for himself if she addresses him. Orel does not like snakes and is unnerved by the coiling ringnecks and coachwhips she keeps in glass cages. There is a dying field mouse being watched, without amusement or appetite, by an ugly hognose.

"I was a wife and had three children," she says, speaking very softly now. "Three little daughters, cute as buttons. Nice little Polish girls, all of them, who went to Catholic school in pretty plaid dresses, and even one who already wore braces. My husband was a radio technician, City of Chicago. I was a music teacher. I always loved Chopin."

She dabs at her damp cheeks and looks her guests over. She follows Lucas's eyes to the glass cages—six in all—and their serpentine inhabitants.

"I don't believe anymore," she says flatly, apparently to Lucas.

"In what?"

She smiles wanly, showing the gray stained teeth of a much older woman, like she has been eating only mud and inky wild berries for years.

"In existence," she murmurs. "I think we're all living in a dream. I *know* we're all living in a dream. Someone's dream … someone real twisted and dark, who hates happiness. We're in that person's dream, and we can't get out of it."

Orel looks over at his father. He had been taking pictures of the snakes, careful not to use his flash. He points at his father's wristwatch when the woman isn't looking. Lucas predicts this woman will be one of the next to go, possibly like Gerard's mother. He wants to joke that the snakes would then die horrible deaths without her around to feed them, but he holds off. They are quickly to another hut and these are people he has yet to meet.

A tall, rail-thin man—with a beard that nearly reaches his belt buckle—answers. His wife is currently sick and does not want to come out of their bedroom to say hello.

"Was that what I think it was?" He asks in a syrupy, Deep South way, as though each word has a life of its own in his mouth. "I've been saying for years … it would be the nuke that would bring our life here to an end. You ask anybody … and they'll tell you … I've been heralding a meltdown … for quite a long time now."

Lucas isn't sure what he has here. The bearded man is about his own age, has clear hazel eyes, appears sober, and has stacks of Chaucer and Shakespeare on a bookshelf between two bright sofas. But the more he talks, the more he comes across as a full-blown dunce.

"We've got maybe a week, tops," Lucas tells him. The bearded man fondly strokes his beard and makes a noise in his throat, but does not say anything. He looks at Orel, who squints through his viewfinder at the slow-witted host. The shutter clicks and all the man does is grin.

"I bet y'all like my beard," he says, smiling so hard that his eyes crinkle to slits.

Lucas begs apology for coming when the wife wasn't feeling well, and the bearded man waves him off, says maybe next time they can all sit around and chat longer.

"You got it," Lucas says, giving his son the go-ahead to start their walk back home.

On the bridge they can see and hear the effects of the meltdown. The water is higher by at least a yard, and it rushes with a purpose; the current has a voice of its own now, louder and more engaged. There's no way you could toss a limb into the current and follow its lazy adventure from stone to stone. Kione stands against the parapet, almost exactly where Lucas put an end to the intruder, and looks out over the churning Haw.

"Well," he calls to Lucas when they get near, "what do we do now, Professor?"

"We have to get our stuff together, plot a course, and head off before the fallout makes its landing on our doorsteps."

Kione flicks a cigarette end over end into the water below and asks if the city would be far enough away.

"I believe it is," answers Lucas. "For those who *can* go back."

Kione purses his lips and nods. Daylight is coming now, a faint gray breach to the dark horizon. There is a guttural cry to the south, where the reactor gushed its guts into sky, soil and stream. It is the lament of some animal racked with pain. Agony.

"The city will go," Kione sighs. "If people don't overrun it with new problems and strains, then the cloud from the nuke will be the end of it. You wait and see if I'm right."

"I'm not arguing against you."

"Hmm. But you will. Later, you will, Lucas. When you're back in that city, you'll protest against the ones like me, the ones who are saying that not only is the end inevitable, but it is here, now."

Lucas remembers his ex-boss, Gail, who echoed this type of pessimism. He wonders if Gail and others like him had something to do with the meltdown. The government has done some horrendous things—intentionally.

But an accident seems more plausible. It could just be a case where the water used to cool the rods had simply gone through enough of a chemical change over the years, so that it reacted with something. The control rods were already wearing down. Maybe the polluted waters took their final toll on them.

"There isn't anywhere to go," Kione says, turning to them.

"Isn't it better in the North?" Lucas asks. "While you can't really trust news on the wires, the environment isn't as violated there as it is here, and out West. Perhaps even Canada, but it would be a lot of trouble to get through the border."

"I'll give you a couple guns," Kione says, "and maybe you and your son could just sneak across the border and keep heading north until you hit clean air and water. Is that what you're thinking?"

"No," Lucas says. "You have to be owners to live above the lines. Come on, you know that. What I'm saying is, we're going to the North. If you want to come with us, all we have to do is stop through the city so I can pick up the rest of our papers."

"You left papers in the city?"

"In a safety box, yes."

Kione laughs. He looks at Orel, then back to Lucas, laughing.

"Just when I think you've got a pretty good head on your shoulders, you want to tell me that you trust the publique?"

"Nobody has any reason to go through my stuff at the public bank. I haven't given the government any strong reason to suspect me, to see that I have done anything other than migrate out on my own. Tens of thousands of people do it every year."

"And all of them are suspected ..." Kione trails off and lights a new cigarette. "Maybe things are different of late. I dunno. You do it your way, Lucas. I'm staying put here. I'll take my chances with the radons or the neutrons or whatever. Black rain, I don't care. I'm going to go out of this world on my own terms."

"So will I."

Kione narrows his eyes and exhales a cloud between them.

"I'm sure you will," he says.

16.

Crowds jam the trains threading into the city on this first day back for workers and students following the calamity at the nuclear reactor. They shout and make their voices hoarse from bellowing curses and threats, with many coming to blows inside the cars and on the platforms before the sun even rises. There is an exodus, as many do not return to their jobs and classes. There is seething resentment toward those who feel the trains should be used for business-as-usual purposes only.

"Clowns!" bellows one man on the downtown route, a Hungarian former professor of philosophy, who is trying to get back to his skyrise after a visit with his children in the North. He shakes his fists at a dark-eyed citoyen who is trying to staunch the flow of trains in and reroute them out, with the hope of bringing thousands of refugees along the way.

The professor, obviously a wayward Hidden (considering the badge that licks out of his topcoat pocket), curls his bony paws at the wrist and strikes at the overgrown citoyen. The refugee—who is desperately seeking to save more than a dozen suffering family, sick with fallout—is in no mood for it. He catches the small professor's arm and snaps it, then grabs the duffer in a headlock and, within seconds, suffocates him.

There are people in the car who applaud the professor's murder. They kick at his crumpled body until it is safely under some seats and no longer in their way.

"Repent!" the citoyen refugee cries as he thrusts his gloved hands to the train ceiling. "Repent! Create freedom with me, Brothers and Sisters!"

By mid-afternoon, military have boarded most city lines, and on two cars they execute outliers who are violently forcing the commuters off. The chaos leaves many workers and students stranded downtown, fearing that if they use the trains to get home they will not make it.

The professor's killer, a hulking brown-skin with long scars across his cheeks, continues to clear seats for refugees, the brothers and sisters of the northbound pilgrimage. In his wake he leaves an entire line of cars bleeding smoke, corpses fanned out from end to end, and a crippling anxiety that the government has lost its hold.

"Repent!"

Graffiti arises as though borne by spores. The locomotives are showered in animal blood, feces and the clothes of the dead as they rumble through ghettos and now-darkened tunnels. Soldiers ride the trains in packs, clogging valuable space just to protect the few who dare board the lines for work and school. The university has threatened to shut down until it is safe again. The government begins housing its workers in apartments and skyrises, forcing the Hidden to double-up in many cases.

"Repent!"

The scarred guerilla—risen to hero status among the people—increases his ranks, to the point that mercenaries are sent after him. In one day he is killed. His kinsman call it a sacrifice, and they carry his giant body, during a downpour, to the columns of the capitol, where they chant his name (they call him *Repent!*) for hours into the night, until somebody releases a volley of bullets into their ranks. Here, the first refugee uprising ends, scattering citoyens in all directions throughout the city.

* * *

Lucas takes his chances and brings Orel and Nico into the city, briefly, before they journey north to meet up with Gerard and Nan. He worries that Nico may not be able to manage his way around if he gets separated from them. He stared hard into Gerard and Nan's eyes as he promised to protect their son, even while knowing—if it's as treacherous in the city as he believes it to be—safety could be elusive.

Their train is jammed. Mean-looking soldiers lumber around in ballistic vests and gas masks, and it is difficult to know who they are watching. Their uniforms are unfamiliar; the guns they clutch are smoking with near-constant use. Lucas and the boys sidestep bodies while boarding at the outskirts, careful to keep time and not bog down the lines—armed commandos barking at anyone who paused to show concern.

Some of those shot are still alive, pleading for help. Some just beg for mercy. On their platform, they see a mother with a hysterical daughter tugging at her wounded arm, until it came off and a sentry steps in to crack the woman's skull with a bludgeon. There is an old man in Arab garb bleeding from his neck as they stand and ride, images of burning neighborhoods and panicked citoyens flickering through the windows. The military now paints the windows black, but someone keeps scraping them clear so that refugees can see in and passengers can see out.

"I want you to keep this," the bleeding Arab wheezes, passing a pocket watch to Nico, who is closest to him in the aisle. "You can remember this was the hour you saw Nasib. A man who was valiant even after the jindy murdered his family. Do not throw it away. Please. It's all that remains of my life."

Nico looks at Orel and Orel turns to his father. Lucas takes the watch from Nico and thanks the dying man. He takes one last look at the time, wraps the chain around the case, and stuffs it inside his coat. Then he looks back to the window where a scraped gash allows him to see fires through the rain. They are rumbling past the old neighborhood and he thinks he sees familiar faces contorted in the clamor there, as the train whizzes past the platform he used to stand on. A bag of blood and vomit hits the window.

Orel taps Lucas on the elbow.

"You're certain they won't find our guns?" he whispers into his ear. "Mine feels like it's falling out of my pocket."

Lucas shakes his head and glances around, sees a riot-gear-masked soldier at the doors they came in through. The soldier is checking the magazine in his weapon and is not watching them.

"It won't come out," he assures Orel, adding: "Pay attention to everybody. Nobody is to be trusted."

As they approach the downtown terminal, the soldiers perk up and start growling at passengers who have fallen asleep or sit slumped in their seats. The Arab is dead. The soldier by the exit comes over and yanks him from his bench, deposits him on the floor and proceeds to kick him until he is certain the Arab is lifeless. Then he lowers his rifle and puts a bullet in Nasib's head.

"Your stop is in thirty seconds," he tells Lucas roughly, catching the bioengineer watching. "I advise you to get yourself ready to depart fast."

They wrap their faces and shuffle with the crowd to the exit sign and brace for the opening of the doors, which happens with a snarl of acrid smoke and the stench of mace, a thundering voice over the intercom robotically ticking off new gate numbers and street exits. Lucas pushes Orel and Nico in the back and they tumble out as a woman screams and hits a soldier in his chest. Unconcerned, the soldier looks at them.

"Keep moving," he mutters.

It is a controlled race up three flights of concrete steps. All the surfaces are either splattered with blood or pocked with bullet marks. At the top of their stairs, behind a trashcan, a rat shivers in a cold wind blowing in off the spines of steel skyrises. Lucas gives directions and they take the inside of the sidewalk, hugging a towering government building. Papers skitter up the sides of the brick edifice, as trash blows into their legs. A few drops of rain spatter their heavy coats.

Lucas signals them to follow him into an alley. He backs behind a nearby dumpster and lays out their plan again, just for his own peace of mind. They have nothing written down and only Lucas carries any documents or identifications—holding on to theirs as well as his own. He explains again that they could get shot—it's practically a given, in fact—if they're searched and their pistols are discovered.

"I will not be gone long," he promises. "I have two trips to make: the bank and the skyrise, right next to each other. It'll be an hour at most."

He has them, in unison, explain what they will do under both scenarios: the one where he gets back safely and the one where he does not. Usually he smiles when he hugs his son, but this time he doesn't. He grabs him, kisses his cheek, and then shoves him away. Nico gets a brief vigorous handshake, and then Lucas is out of the alley and back down the sidewalk, head lowered against the wind.

* * *

Gail stands at a window, gazing across the rooftops, then the narrow chugging stripes of the railway tracks and the liquid refuse that pours through low side streets, and then off farther out to the specks which are certainly the throngs of refugees closing in on the heart of the city.

He lets his phone ring on the desk behind him, until it stops and his button begins to chirp. There will be a knock on his door before too long. They cleared out the floor below yesterday, shuffling off bleary-eyed power and utilities managers, some literally being tossed into the street to make their own way from here on out. The rest were transited to other parts of the city, or put out of it altogether. There is always consolidation to think of. If you are chosen, you accept without a word. This fellow, Juda, who keeps swinging by his office asking about one of the bioengineers, will be brought over before the day ends. They seem curious about him. Gail finds the Transportation department ill fitted to be held in such esteem. Their task is ordinary, could be handled through software. He is supposed to handle Juda without tipping him off, somehow detaining the man while they decide his fate.

Whoever has been calling, stops. There is a knock at his door. It grows urgent by the third series. Gail opens it to a brown man of medium height and build, a well-dressed member of the Transportation wing. Juda swabs at his brow and forces a smile.

"I had to walk up all those stairs," Juda explains, making note that the man invites him in coldly, does not offer his hand. "Pardon me for sweating."

Gail says it is not unusual for people to sweat these days, even profusely. Times are such that conditions are deteriorating rapidly. Nerves are frayed. Glands are overtaxed.

"You can sit facing the window," he offers to his guest, bored with this already, and irritated that the man whom he is to keep calm and captive—maybe for hours—shows up a mess. "We can soon have lunch. Preferences?"

Juda says no, fidgets with his tie, smiles nervously.

"I think I'm catching a cold," he says.

* * *

Orel takes Nico to the plaza, which is out in the open and the elements, but has an almost sacred standing with the military. You won't get shot here, probably not even beaten. As such, it is crowded to the point of absurdity. They're squeezed in so that elbows thrust into ribs and only the tallest seem comfortable, able to breathe. The mob sucks at the foul air without protection, and many seem sick.

Nico points to a far corner of the plaza where barrel fires glow and angry men in heavy coats glare at all the entrances. This is where the protectors for the refugees have made camp. Orel says they shouldn't go over. It's too dangerous.

"There may soon be a killing spree," he hisses over the din. Nico nods. He asks if they can leave the plaza now that they have seen it. It is too cold and there are too many people. A young boy with a can of spray paint runs over and asks if they want to huff—only a small fee. His hands are smeared with dull-gold paint, as are his nose and mouth. He takes a dead snake from his cargo pants pocket and tosses it onto the pavement, then drops to his knees and flecks the scaly carcass with a buttery mist.

"You can buy this gold snake now?" asks the boy, who trembles uncontrollably. His stare is somewhere between them, as if his vision is poor. Orel shakes his head and they start to go, aware now that the crowd continues to swell and that someone is talking loudly about getting a group to storm the capitol, right at the columns. The speaker contends that they are enough of a body to force their way inside. Others grumble along, and when a pair of soldiers come strolling through one of the entryways behind Orel and Nico, a shout goes up.

"Find me later," the boy says quickly, thrusting his paint and dead snake back into his pants. He is all knees and elbows as he flees, squeezing past the legs of jeering citoyens who are, as one, jabbing their fists into the wet sky.

Orel grabs Nico and shoves him toward their corridor, ducking as they run because now there are shots fired and people are scattering, screaming, and it is all they can do to reach the opening. It leads them back to where they stood with Lucas behind the dumpster, just yards from the terminal. Nico's eyes are wild with fright. In his panic, he has grabbed his pistol and he points it shakily at the entrance to their alley.

"Are you crazy?" Orel gasps, snatching the Beretta before anyone sees it. He pockets it in his own coat and feels sorry for taking Nico away from Gerard and Nan and his brothers. Orel hugs Nico, to feel his warmth and his love, suddenly aware that each minute could be their last.

* * *

Lucas peers through the dark glass into the bank. He uses his badge to slip through a side entry, a government workers' passage, and keeps his head low as he walks quickly along the camera-heavy tunnel. He has no idea why his badge still works, and he hopes there's no government endgame to draw him in, as far as he can go, until a trap is sprung. An eerie hush permeates the place. No longer are there fake trees in planters or soapy jazz chords washing through the heated lobby.

A guard with a strapped rifle stops him at the last glass door. He asks for papers, and Lucas unfolds his identification. The guard nods and goes back to looking out through a series of glass walls to the street, where people are moving hurriedly in one direction—toward the plaza.

"You should go ahead and take it all out," the guard calls after him. "Every bit of it. This place is going to hell any day now."

Inside, the tellers are working out of a labyrinth of steel plates and armed guards. An old woman in a pink trench coat with a fur collar turns and eyes him suspiciously. There's a mastiff on a rope at the end of her arm. Lucas flashes his badge again, flaps his papers for a pair of bank clerks, and is led through the tube to the depository. The lighting is strange, as if mercury vapors were in use again, and now he can hear a conversation coming from the sound system. One man is talking to another about the benefits of donating large amounts of cash to the government, which in turn gives secure credit down the line.

"Tomorrow never happens without today," the main voice, a cheery nasal Midwestern accent, intones.

Lucas waits in the tube, noticing how the luster of the enamel on the outer tiles is still brilliant. It reminds him of something his father used to say about how a kingdom that prospers will function like a kingdom, while a kingdom that fails will only look like one—or something to that effect. He looks back out the tube to see if there's anybody coming in who could spot him and alert the guards to his status.

"Here you go," the valet says, handing Lucas his box. "There's an extra key here," he points under the box, "and you may want to take it off and put it somewhere safe."

Lucas thanks him and hurries back up the tube, through the strange cubicles where dozens of tellers work furiously to empty accounts, and then back into the lobby. The same guard is still keeping watch on the street. He touches his helmet as Lucas goes past.

"Come back and see us," he says with a laugh.

Outside, the wind is colder and it rains in earnest, rushing through gutters and pipes. Though muted by the rain, he can hear a cacophony rising in the plaza. He hopes Orel and Nico are not there. They are supposed to be back at the dumpster in forty minutes.

* * *

Juda is surprised that they are bringing lunch to him. He figures this is their bizarre way of firing him, as so many in his office were let go over the past few days. There are stories of being accosted in the bathroom (during bowel movements, no less) or being followed onto the elevator to be told you were fired. But there are no tales of tasty meals during the deed.

"What can you tell me about the trains?" Gail asks. "When will they be safe to ride again?"

Juda pushes his fork through a tender maze of cheese and marinara, waiting to see how deep it goes before he strikes eggplant.

"Excuse me?"

"All this violence and disorder with the trains—when's it going to stop?"

"Oh. I thought that's what you asked. I just don't know. I can't find anybody who knows. Sometimes I wonder if anybody even wants to find out."

"I do. I want to find out."

Juda raises his eyes and sees Gail is staring out the window. Disinterested, or perhaps having memories.

"I really *don't* know," Juda says quietly.

Gail touches his ear and transfers his gaze from one sheet of glass to the next. Juda turns and looks over his shoulder but cannot find anything that could possibly hold his own interest like this.

"There isn't anything like a good eggplant parmesan," Gail muses, though he has not touched his food. "My uncle married an Italian woman."

Juda shrugs. It is good to know there are still some fantastic places to eat in the city, is what he wants to say. He also wants to ask what their meeting is about, and if it's possible that he's never going to find out, since it looks like they just got together for lunch and small talk.

"I think that was very wise of your uncle," Juda says.

Gail smiles faintly and starts drumming the arms of his chair.

"My uncle used to drive one of these trains. An engineer on one of the lines ... I think it was the line from the west to the lake. What was that line called? He used to say it all the time ... 'The blank line, I'm going to be dreaming about the blank line in my grave.' The blank line. I'll never remember it. But it was the line my uncle engineered for forty, maybe fifty years."

"Sounds like a good man."

"He was."

Juda rests his plate gently on the coffee table and wipes the corners of his mouth. He looks out the windows to where Gail keeps his sentinel. They're facing west, and maybe a little south. The rain drills the glass, pushing waves down as fast as they will run. And there in the distance, as far as the eye can see, a tiny red dot blinks.

17.

Gerard tries securing the pen with wire, which has always been a problem due to rust and the fact that metals do not give and take when the winds whip up. Wire has been known to collapse the posts and let the goats and chickens run around the hillside until a stray bobcat comes along and puts an end to their freedom.

So he goes with rope. It will rot over time, but in the short term it rarely fails. Kione and Drake are down at the tank, feeding the Coho, putting the bone meal to work. Their thinking is these salmon will reach maturity in a few months, at least to the point where they can feed people. Kione says a few months is too long and they are wasting their time. He says anyone who wants to live should be pulling out within two weeks, once the goats and chickens start to die.

"We're going to starve before we can have a decent pan-fried supper," he told them, even before they took the pieces of the slain intruder and ground them into meal. "The radioactive contamination will take hold within days. There is already an organized evacuation out of here, maybe tens of thousands on the roads. If you wait too long, you won't be able to get out."

Eddie Drake says he is not going anywhere. "I'll stay with the fish," he tells Kione, as Gerard comes in the geodesic and they watch the water swirl and foam as the salmon feed. "I got no chance on the highway."

Who does? This is what Gerard wants to know. Nan has been packing and she already grieves for Nico, not knowing whether he made it to the city with Lucas and Orel. She wants to go north and says their best chance is to follow Lucas.

"I'm hearing the military is shooting at will," Drake says agitatedly. "Indiscriminately. You have maybe a million refugees already, by most counts. Likely more. And where are they going?"

Kione, drained of motivation, scoops out a fry and lets it hop and twist in his palm. He touches its silver head with his index finger, then tosses it back into the tank and wipes his hands on his coveralls. He looks at Gerard, who is climbing the ladder to join them on the scaffold.

"Me and Hocus Pocus are going to stay behind," he says, "regardless of who goes. I can't assure anyone that I won't get arrested and he ... Eddie thinks he has a future in aquaculture."

"I do, like Jesus did," Drake says.

Gerard frowns.

"If Nan goes, I go. Simple as that. It's what happens."

There is a sharp wind against the window, the steel panels shake, and a tree outside snaps and falls and they feel it strike the earth. Drake spits in the water and wags a finger to make a point.

"All the bills are coming due," he says. "All of them."

"We're planning on leaving first light tomorrow," Gerard announces, ignoring the old man's ramblings. "Heading out north, right along with everybody else."

They plan to take their truck, a heavily modified dinosaur that Nan claims can breathe and think on its own. It is an eight-wheel behemoth that gets forty miles to the gallon on kitchen oils. Cyril and Torrey are cramming essentials into the cargo bed while Bixby watches. The dog is aware that Nico is not around, but he stays occupied with the smaller boys. He barks when the walnut tree topples.

The men stare into the tank and discuss the crippled nuke site. Helicopters are in and out of the sky above, all manner of aircraft could be heard spraying nearby forests with limb-shattering rounds, total annihilation of some pocket of humanity deemed malignant to the others.

Nan talks to Nico on her button, while he is still on the train heading into the city. There is some hope they can meet up with him on the freeway outside of D.C. She promises they will have Bixby when they meet him.

* * *

Lucas scours the façade for some indication as to where he can enter. These skyrises are all so impenetrable, he marvels at the discretion and mystery that has gone into them. He remembers the archaeologists who first entered the tombs of the pharaohs, how focused they were despite such bewildering premises.

These buildings are pure fortresses, honed like mausoleums, guarded with the best weaponry and technology available. Lucas thinks it's sad that they are used for no other purpose than to protect wealthy Hidden from the inevitable rebellion they inspire.

He runs his hands over the smooth stonework, closes his eyes to heighten his tactile approach. There's a crack that runs in a jagged diagonal; it splits into branches and finally moves on, and up, beyond his reach. He opens his eyes to see where it goes. Despite a fine mist that wets his eyelashes and hisses against the stones, he follows the steady ascension of the crack, to a pilaster that is topped by a leering winged gargoyle. It's impossible to reach.

So he moves around the corner of the building, careful to watch down the alleys. But there's nobody there, just dripping and oozing rainwater, and the echoes from violence in the plaza. There are usually armed guards scowling through clear visors—on the lookout for ragged citoyens panhandling around the skyrises. Right now, they've left for other places, presumably the plaza. Lucas waits for someone to come, anyone, it doesn't matter. The Hidden will have to break their convention. He squats in a recess between marble pillars and thinks of what it will be like to get out of here. If they're right about a fraction of the North, it will provide plenty—more than enough. That choice seems solid.

The woman in the pink trench coat from the bank, hurries past him, not seeing Lucas because her giant mastiff obscures him there, crouched against the building. The dog swings its head and growls. Lucas comes out of his crouch and aims his pistol at her, just as she turns to look. She pouts. He expects a scream or at least a gasp of fright, but her only expression is one of inconvenience.

"You'll never make it back out," she warns in a voice creaky with age and cigarettes. He says nothing, just wags his pistol for her to lead him in.

"Suit yourself," she snaps.

Inside, the ventilation noise surprises him. It's a habitat unto itself. The wet mastiff sneezes, sending echoes far up through hidden chambers and vaulted ceilings that follow a central elevator system. The old woman stares at him.

"What are you waiting for?" she asks sharply. "Why can't you just shoot me so I can go ahead and let Kline get upstairs? I'd rather my dog live than me, just in case I have any choice in what's going to happen."

Lucas keeps his barrel leveled at her as he gets in the elevator.

"A lot is going to happen," he says as he presses the button to close the doors. "Make your choices wisely." Then he grabs one door to hold it open for a moment. He thinks maybe the look on her face might change, but it remains frozen in haughtiness. She's like an old painting of a queen. Her eyes are fearless. He figures they've never shown fear.

"Does a man named Pavla still live here?" he asks quickly, before her dog erupts or soldiers burst in through some side doors.

"Ha!" she laughs. "Find him yourself."

He lets the doors close but he can still see her, standing there, through a slot in the doors. She still has that expression, her face smeared with disdain and, perhaps, disappointment. He turns around until he finds another porthole that offers him a view out the back. For maybe twenty floors, he can see nothing, and then the world below opens up, offered stunningly through the glass upper-half of the skyrise. He presses against the back wall, straining to see what he needs to recognize down there: the terminal, the plaza, and the tracks leading north out of the city. There is red smoke in the plaza, the sign of military aggression. It spirals up and kisses the glass of his skyrise. He can tell nothing from his view of the terminal, other than that it isn't choked with smoke, red or otherwise. At present, there is a black train snaking through

scorched warehouses, all of its cars intact, accelerating away
from the terminal.

Slowly he becomes aware that there is music draining
through the speakers in the ceiling. It is the same orchestral
electronica piped into the trains and libraries. There is also a
whiff of peppermint in the air, which he remembers from the
last time he was in here, years before. But that was a sad visit,
just after Sila died. Lucas recalls a happier trip here, to pick up
the keys to Sila's beloved new car.

The elevator stops abruptly and the door opens with a
hiss. He walks to one end of the hallway and looks out the
glass. The view is dizzying, easily a thousand feet up. From
here, Lucas can see the distant plume of the crippled nuclear
reactor, the smoldering beds of wasteland citoyen slums, and
even the dome at the airport where the government readies for
its own evacuation. There is a solid chrome door to his right.
He recognizes the curvy symbol on it, but has forgotten what it
stands for—what Pavla said it meant. He removes a plastic
card from his box and inserts it in the slot below the symbol.
He waits.

After a while, he slumps on the floor and dozes for
several minutes, knowing it may take the old man ages to
summon the energy to answer. In the meantime, there is the
pink lady downstairs. She is definitely the type who will call
security. They could be clambering aboard the elevator at any
moment, this woman chirping away at them that vandals are a
breach of her contract and that she may have to take her
wealth elsewhere. He fantasizes that they shoot her, or at the
very least gas her a bit, before they rise to apprehend their
intruder.

The chrome door opens. Just a slice of darkness appears
in the jamb where the old man peers out.

"Who's there?"

Lucas scrambles to his feet and starts talking, reminding a
deep-set watery eye that he is the one who married Sila, and
how kind he, Lucas, was when the old uncle was grieving over
his niece's tragic death.

"I've come back for her bones," Lucas finishes. "The
ones that you have, Uncle Pavla."

Pavla's milky eye vanishes and the door rocks in just enough for Lucas to squeeze through. There's endless white carpet and walls, like an art gallery, or the inside of a sugar cube. A white cat with lime-green eyes and endless fluffs of hair dozes on the hearth in front of a gas fire. The old man is listening to classical music on a flawless Dolby. To Lucas, it feels like the notes are forming from within his own head.

"Sila," Uncle Pavla mumbles as he sinks into a chair cushion, "broke many hearts."

Lucas pauses before he sits opposite the retired scientist. Pavla looks a hundred years old, and is frail to the point of disintegrating into his own folded skin. The hands are nothing but sinewy fingers and discolorations. His silver hair is disheveled, and when he lays an oversized pair of glasses on the bridge of his nose, he becomes comical.

"She was special," Lucas admits, as if they were discussing her in front of television cameras for a news segment, "one of the rarest of people."

Pavla nods sadly and gazes at his Persian. He reaches into his shirt pocket and removes a strip of something that requires further unwrapping. Once he has removed the cellophane, he smells it, expanding his lungs and sighing out as if it is some fragrant delicacy.

"Here, Portia," he says to the cat. "Here, my lovely."

But the cat doesn't budge, won't even flinch as Pavla wags the savory treat. He smiles at Lucas.

"Lazy," he chuckles. There is a reflection from the licking fire in his glasses and Pavla seems to grow transfixed with it on his lenses.

"Uncle Pavla," Lucas says as he leans forward, aware of the time. "Do you still have Sila's bones?"

Pavla scratches his face, which is spattered with white whiskers. His eyes flutter and his bottom lip droops, the mannerisms of a sad child. He drums the arms of his chair and looks around.

"Somewhere," he says wistfully. "Everything is somewhere, isn't that right?"

This man was a member of the nuclear engineering team that sought to dismantle the old nuke sites in favor of newer ones. But it was a matter of money, and saving money always wins. He is one of the few who was placed in a skyrise by the government, costing him nothing. He said it was a reward for keeping his mouth shut and allowing the world to descend into madness.

"I want to take the bones with me," explains Lucas, being patient with his wife's old uncle, who helped them buy their first car when Sila needed one for lecturing at universities throughout the South.

"Finally," Pavla smiles, "things are starting to come full circle?"

Lucas doesn't know what this means and he makes a face to show it. Pavla is a bachelor who traveled at the start of his career, spending time in New Zealand, Nova Scotia, California and the Canadian badlands, pouring his knowledge and skills into the projects that would connect the world's nuclear power grid.

But not long after Lucas married his niece, Pavla was scandalized at work, like so many others—either at the whim of a superior, or simply by not seeming loyal enough. He resorted to teaching, overseeing existing sites, babying lesser minds, all things that appeared to bring him little joy. And then one night during a summer dinner at Lucas and Sila's little house in the city, Pavla smacked his forehead, as if doing a shtick from an old movie. Lucas would later say it surprised him the man didn't bellow "Eureka!"

Pavla worked back in the labs for a while, wearing his white coat again, running his hands through his thick (and then-black) hair, mumbling to himself and others about some theory that could change the way power is made. It didn't work. He was relegated back to classrooms and dusty diagrams and maps, twiddling his thumbs.

And he became a worrier who warned of obvious tribulations, outliving his usefulness before even turning sixty. He said he would become a painter or a sculptor in retirement. He had his artist friend come to his penthouse—a prize even for the wealthiest of the Hidden—and give lessons to him and his niece. Sila was at her happiest then and that's when she became pregnant.

"I haven't been out in years," the old man concedes, playing with something between his fingers in his lap. "It's like I've died but I'm still alive. It is strange. But who doesn't know that?" He snaps feebly at his cat, but Portia only interrupts her dozing to glance at him. "For a very long time, I have felt that I would have been better off dead. You should hear the way some of us talk. Those of us up on these higher floors, all we do is complain. The tedium is maddening. What are we waiting for? There are some who ask that. *What are we waiting for?* But you know that nobody has the answer to that. It sounds like a good question at first. But it has become an annoyance."

He looks across to one of his enormous windows and points.

"Things are not so good out there, are they?"

Lucas shakes his head. The man gave him and his wife a tiny Rembrandt as a wedding gift. It was lost in the fire.

"We are maybe days from the end," says Lucas.

"Good. Not so much for you, but for me. This fellow on the floor below me, he's always chatting about suicide. He never takes himself up on it though. Just chats about it."

Lucas decides it is time to mention the purpose of his visit again. He quickly explains about Orel, the trains going north, and the mobs in the plaza and on the freeways, the whole bit.

"I should tell the fellow on the floor below me," Pavla grins. "He'll get a kick out of it."

18.

Orel pushes back into the space between the dumpster and the wall, pressing Nico behind him, until there is a groan. He holds the pistol ready.

A man and a woman stagger into the alley, the man clutching his stomach. They are dirty and wild, clothed in a mix of rags and old military gear. The woman has a chevron on her shoulder that identifies her as a master sergeant. She holds the man against her, bending her knees to steady him as he bleeds steadily through his fingers.

"God can rot!" he snarls, twisting his head this way and that. He has a full beard, though some of it is burned off. One of his ears is missing. She tries to see out of the alley, but a cloud of choking black smoke drifts down the street

"Hang on," she whispers into his proper ear, rubbing gently at his beard where it's not charred away.

The man shakes and blood squirts through his hand. His boots slip on the wet pavement and he collapses under her, cursing as he falls. She hugs his neck and whispers, keeps telling him to hang on. Out of the smoke, a military enforcer appears, his gray armor smeared with bits and pieces of flesh. He wields a smooth wide blade in one hand, a powerful submachine gun in the other. The woman screams and he shoots her until she crashes into the wall, twisting into a strange fetal position. The injured man fires from a mini shotgun that rocks the soldier, but does not bring him down.

"Do it! Do it!" the man yells, trying to load another muzzle rocket. His hands so bloody that he drops the fat shell between his legs. The soldier slashes his blade across the man's face and sends the top half of his head flying down the alley toward the dumpster. The man slumps back against the woman's coiled body.

The soldier scans, reloading. He is grabbed from the smoke by another armored form and disappears, apparently firing down the street toward the terminal entrance where screams are now rising in unison.

"We'll never get out of here," Nico whispers, shaking. The ground rumbles as if someone has detonated a bomb within the train tunnels. Orel rises halfway and throws back a side door to the dumpster and peers in. Seeing nothing but trash, he scrambles inside and helps Nico tumble in as well. They slide the door back and wait in the darkness for Lucas to return.

* * *

Gerard and Nan have said their goodbyes to the farm and the life they are leaving behind. They put the truck on the highway at daybreak, just as the rain stops and a heavy fog spreads, a seething mist that rises from the Haw and its countless collector creeks and streams. Gerard flips on all the lights—the yellow orbs atop the cab, as many eyes as a spider—and they climb the hillside out of their valley. There are cars chugging along at low speeds; some are broken down on the easements, their occupants waving at passersby. The truck is passed almost at once by a roaring four-by-four that swerves through traffic, a cloaked lunatic waving a shotgun at every vehicle, from his perch atop the truck bed—a plastic chair bolted to a platform that is used to hunt deer at long range, across fields.

"Look at that," Gerard murmurs, gripping the wheel tightly.

They take side roads that loop back and forth between freeways and dirt paths. Gerard has ventured far and wide to raise and trade goats, so he knows the outlying landscape like few others. He says this route will help to avoid gatherings where "evil gets done or the evil get dead." There's a smoldering forest behind a covered bridge, where a farmer used to live. He and his family produced thousands of fresh eggs every morning. They worked in the dark, every day for years, despite the weather and the violence that could spill out from the city, using a ghost story similar to the one used by the peaceniks in Bynum.

"He was another man," Gerard explains as he scans the horizon, "who relied on fear of the occult—the legend and the myth of it—to keep prying hands and minds away."

Nan watches a girl beside the road, who is maybe twelve, standing under a willow tree. The girl is watching traffic as she cuts her own hair with large shears. Beside her is a man on his knees, praying.

"Those days are over," Nan sighs. "You won't be able to scare away people anymore. They've all given up on religion so many times now, there's no religion to give up anymore. And you have to have religion to make people fear the devil. I mean, when was the last time you heard of someone getting in trouble for worshipping Satan?"

He shrugs. "It's been a while, I guess."

"Sure it has. It has been a damn helluva long while. Nobody cares anymore."

"Maybe they've just stopped worshipping Satan?" Gerard says.

Nan clucks her tongue. "They still worship the devil," she counters. "People have been worshipping the devil almost as long they've prayed to God."

"Maybe longer?"

"Maybe even longer, Baby."

On their sweep far to the south of the city, they approach a camper with smoke oozing from its popped hood. The camper is on a road that exits a public lake. A couple in cowboy hats are waving bandanas at them.

"You think it's safe?" Nan asks. She has an automatic rifle in her lap. Gerard wags his head and says there will be a steady stream of vehicles, maybe even a few mechanics, coming along this road today. He waves at the couple, whose faces melt into frowns as the big ugly truck rumbles by.

"It doesn't help our karma," Gerard says with a sigh. "But there's no risk when you don't stop."

Before they left, Kione strolled in to say his goodbyes. He held onto a near-empty bottle of whiskey and said he'd spent most of the night at the snake woman's house, listening to her old records.

"It's a surprise to myself," he chuckled when Nan lifted her eyebrow. "Lots of old music can put you in a weird mood, a nostalgic mood even. It was a very nostalgic night. Seeing good people like you leave makes me kinda nostalgic. But I wish you all the best, even so."

And then he laid the law down for Gerard: no Good Samaritan routines, no rolling through checkpoints without an exit strategy, shoot if you have to, etc. He suggested not stopping when switching drivers.

"Just hop across the seat," he grinned drunkenly, "like they did on the stagecoaches."

Remembering Kione's words, Nan puts her rifle back under her seat and agrees with Gerard.

"Five hours before D.C.," she says, noticing a red light in her rear-view, sort of back off from where they just came. She figures it's a fire truck and that the couple outside the camper will soon be back on the road.

* * *

Lucas props up the fatigued Uncle Pavla as they walk into the kitchen. There are floor-to-ceiling windows beside a wide marble table on which stand several potted orchids, each one marking its unique spot in the cluster. Pavla points to the flowers and says he got them when Sila died.

"They're remarkably vigilant," he says as he lowers himself into a chair at the table where he can look out over the city. He instructs Lucas how to make some coffee, and says he remembers now that his guest was coming for the bones of his dead wife. There is more smoke below, in the streets, and bleeding from buildings—including the terminal. At the airport, now barely visible through a window, planes are landing in succession. There are jets circling in the sky above. Lucas fears there will be a *closing of the hole*, as it's called, an ever shrinking window of opportunity. Pavla sees he's fretting and suggests they take their coffee into his gallery, just off the kitchen.

"Let me show you some old things we made," he says, "and then I will give you her bones. I know you're in a hurry.

It is bad out there, is it not? Everything comes full circle now? I hear that doomsday is upon us."

His gallery is just that: floors of polished tan wood, lighting screwed into walls and recessed across the ceiling, and white pedestals on which stand both human figures and abstract forms. On the walls are a series of black-and-white photographs (it reminds Lucas of Orel), and a few impressionist landscapes, which Pavla goes to first.

"My grandfather painted these," he says, going close to the canvases. "He was maybe twenty and it was just before he left Belgium. He would go back ... you can still go back? You can? Well, he would return and say each time it was no different. Not like here and so many other places. He said it was as if time itself would come through Belgium to rest, as it raced around the rest of the world. Here he has painted a man sitting in a garden, down in the front, who rests and reads a book of poetry. I know it is poetry because he told me it was. Time is at leisure. Can you imagine that? Can we stop time now, in this way, now that we have set the clock to expire upon us?"

Lucas fiddles with the wing of an angel on a thin figurine, wondering if the old man will stop talking and just hand over the bones, if he topples the sculpture. He gave Pavla these bones, these bits of Sila that the government felt compelled to return to him, because the uncle has secure places. They say that the homes of the Hidden are filled with family relics—treasures in some cases, bizarre artifacts in others.

"Do you have any news for me other than to report the end is close? Has there been any unexpected turn or twist of fate?"

Pavla stands with his shoulders stooped, tugging gently at the corners of his mouth. He bobs his head and puts his hand up so that Lucas does not have to keep struggling to find answers. He steps lightly over to one of the sculptures—a circular ceramic piece that must be a globe, though none of the continents are familiar. The old man wraps his bony fingers around the globe and lifts it carefully. It appears to be light.

"I made this one on my own," Pavla says quietly as the cat tiptoes into the gallery, suddenly interested. "It isn't very appealing. I am aware of that."

There is an explosion in the city that gently tremors the windows and walls, clinks some of the dishes in the kitchen. They cannot see because the window is not visible to them, but a snarling column of smoke emerges from the capitol and within seconds the plaza is on fire with burning citoyens.

Pavla hands Lucas the globe.

"Your bones," he whispers. Hesitating only for a slight second, Lucas quickly breaks the globe open to get the bones out. Pavla winces, his last link to Sila breaking apart, as Lucas removes a felt bag from the shards. Lucas gently tightens the felt around the bones and says he has to go.

The old man accepts thanks with a two-handed shake, bowing his head slightly, eyes on the broken ceramic shards scattered across the floor. He says he wishes he had more to give. Lucas smiles and arranges the straps of his bag onto his shoulders. Inside is a mesh wire case for the bones, and the box with all their papers. A few shards from the globe get tossed in.

"For luck and memory," Pavla grins.

He takes the elevator down, watching the burning city rise around him. At the ground floor, the doors hiss open and there are a few strange, wild-eyed people in the lobby. Older Hidden, perhaps in anguish or possibly waiting for escorts out. The woman in the pink trench coat sits on a bench beside a magnificent bust of Aristotle. Her dog is gone. She stares at the tile floor and casually smacks a pair of pink leather gloves into her palm.

Lucas walks past her on his way out.

"Hey," she mumbles to him. "You let me know if you see my Kline out there. He jumped right out my window. Eighty floors up, and he goes out like he is a bird and can fly."

A young bald-headed man with sharp cheekbones stands beside her. Her escort. These are former military like Kione, often homicidal, fairly cunning, and—like this tall paladin—armed with weaponry that looks confusing to use. He shakes his head and motions for Lucas to keep walking.

"Did you open the window?" the woman says to her escort. "I know I didn't. I haven't been able to get that thing open for years. You must have done it because Kline didn't do it. And I didn't do it. My hands haven't been such that I could open that window for years. This whole time that I've had Kline, I've never opened that window."

Lucas pushes out the door and is hit by the gusty, smoky wind, the roaring bedlam close by, and the wet cold air that pushes deeper into the skin—almost to the bone—than it ever has before. He takes one last look up the side of the skyrise, where its tower needles into the low clouds and disappears, hoping that Pavla's peace is swift and everlasting.

19.

A number of years before, there was a team of young scientists who gathered for lunch every Friday to review the week almost behind them. When he had more hair and a bit of a tan, Gail was one of them. They sat around a table in the atrium and swapped stories, read each other's reports, caught up on fledgling families, and sometimes boasted about whose kayaking trips were the most impressive.

There were no taboos about internal powwows then. They didn't have to sign off on electronic pledges, or record in secret when speaking with a colleague who maybe shouldn't be trusted. Gail charmed his fellow biologists and engineers. There was outward no sign yet of the man who would one day storm down a fluorescent green hallway and threaten to kill them, their families, and anybody who knew them.

They would sometimes push their table into filtered sunlight and debate who had taken the best vacation that summer. Gail told them about an upcoming trip he was taking to China, on what was known as a '*workcation*'. He was part of a team being sent to Guangdong for two months. The environmental toll there was massive, and world governments scrambled their best and brightest to figure out how to keep it from happening within their borders. Gail was part of a second or third wave to visit the coal-choked coast and inland regions.

He stayed in a side-street hotel with a small outdoor pool, a shadowy dive bar, and several Han girls who came and went at all hours. During the day, his team did next to nothing, mostly just sat around sipping tea and checked their buttons for news from home. There seemed to be a mix-up, a delay in the presentations they'd come to see. The U.S. kept telling them to bide their time as best they could. The Chinese just ignored them. For three weeks it was a rotating farce: boredom, shuffling in and out of tea houses, more boredom, and then a few bits of warning about sulfur dioxide.

Gail spent his weekend nights carousing with some of the other experts, including a pair from Wyoming who were early into their careers as climatologists.

"We need to be able to tell them something when we get back," the broad-shouldered MIT alum, Sandy, said. "Even if it's made up."

The other one was a young German-born woman with nervous eyes, thin lips that were always painted burgundy, and a quiet cough.

"The Chinese," Maxine explained, "make no apologies for what they have done. I am not sure what our countries expect to learn here."

Gail told them he had heard a few insights in previous seminars, but nothing breathtaking. They agreed they would wait patiently for illumination, and if none came, so be it. China was still a bewitching place and they could entertain themselves for another five weeks. They took drives to the mountains and temples, toured the Pearl River at night (drunk to blindness) in a sampan, scoured seedy bars for misfits and irregulars, and rested on the pebbly South China Sea beaches to recover from it all.

Maxine became restless after another week of it and said she had called the home office in Cody (news that unsettled and depressed Sandy) and told them it was turning out to be a huge waste of time.

"Suit yourself," Gail said, making a note to never underestimate Maxine.

He started hanging around the basement bar of his hotel, reluctant to team up with Sandy, who always became too drunk and had to be helped around, and then dropped back into his bed in the morning. He got to know the staff and was curious who these Han girls were who streamed in and out, wearing what appeared to be costumes for a Broadway musical or maybe an opera. There was nothing traditional about it. And they were not prostitutes, he was told that first week.

One Sunday night he was lingering at a small dark table near the back, drooped over a glass of huangjiu, listening to a punk band made up of two people: an out-of-tune guitar and snare drum. The drunken band yelped about taking a break, and someone applauded. The guitarist came over and sat at Gail's table, grinning broadly like they were old buddies from college.

"They want you to dance," the kid—he couldn't have been out of his teens yet—said, laughing at the end. And he pointed out across the bar, with its crowd of maybe six others. Gail shook his head. "Yes! They say you a real good dancer and you must dance for our next song."

Gail took a drink and eyed the kid who had a silver loop ring in both cheeks, heavy on the eye makeup, and a shock of electric-blue hair right down the middle.

"I haven't seen a Mohawk in years," Gail told the guitarist. He apologized and said he could not dance because he had a very inflamed blister on the bottom of one foot. It was on the verge of becoming infected, he went on. It's the sort of thing that happens when you're always concerned about staying in line and marching with the rest of the band, especially if that band is the United States Government.

The kid frowned and ran a hand through his Mohawk, looked around for his drummer and signaled it was time to get back to it.

"I'll play you a song then," the kid said, laughing at the end. "What song is your favorite?"

Gail emptied his glass and made a signal to the bar for another. The bartender was a surly older woman with a square face and bad teeth. She was always reading news on her button when she had the chance.

"*Love Will Tear Us Apart*," Gail said. "Greatest song ever. Of any genre."

The kid nodded and smacked his thighs. He and the drummer leaned their heads together for a second and then launched into the song, which sounded ridiculous. And it was right about here that Maxine came in, her face white, no lipstick on, her hands trembling like an old person's. She sat and took the drink from the surly barmaid and drank it half down in a gulp.

"War," Maxine croaked, wiping her mouth. "The U.S. is at war."

"With who?"

"We have to go back. Tonight."

"Christ, Maxine, with who?"

Maxine looked at the punk band and made a face.

"They are god awful," she said, loud enough for everybody to hear.

*   *   *

When Gail tells Juda not to worry, he means it.

"Are you certain?" Juda says, really feeling like he is coming down with something now. Maybe a cold, or maybe the flu, which can be brought on by stress. Juda glances at the window and wants to say something about all the fires and the smoke and the guns. It feels silly for him to say nothing.

"We will have all this straightened out by tomorrow," Gail says, smoothing his pants and jacket as he stands to escort Juda out. The interrogation is over. "No need to worry."

*   *   *

That last night in Guangzhou, he and Maxine decided to make it memorable. They clinked glasses and cheered the horrible punk duo. They tossed their company credit cards onto the bar and said the sky was the limit, why not? Maxine called Sandy and told him to get out of his room and onto the streets with them. Last night!

They spilled into the neon streets and staggered, three across and arm in arm, laughing and singing like they were sailors from an old wartime movie. They stopped and watched a street opera unfold, magical masked dancers and hidden drums and flutes—the allure of a suggested tiger which was about to leap out and maim the virginal heroine.

"The classic damsel in distress," cried Maxine.

They sat on the wall of a fountain and listened to the water. There were no children in it at this hour. Sandy took off his shoes and socks and soaked his feet. An old man on the opposite side scowled at this and said something in Cantonese. Gail took out his tablet and started looking for news on the wire. Maxine rested her hand on the glass.

"Don't do it," she pleaded. "Not right now, anyway. We've got the whole flight back."

Sandy splashed his feet in the water and suggested they go to the convention center, first thing in the morning, and let them know. Maybe grab a free breakfast at the same time. They decided it could be fun to sit through one last lecture and perhaps heckle the presenter. Everybody had fantasized about doing it, hadn't they?

Gail said he wanted to make a final run to the beach. Just spend another afternoon watching the green sea undulate through the haze, drink until sunset, and then drive back and board the last flight out before midnight.

"That old guy," Sandy whispered out of the corner of his mouth, drunkenly, "is up to something."

The night ended at sunrise inside a smoky theater with the three of them watching a comedy filmed right after the advent of sound. A couple of Italian goofballs were pranking everyone in sight. Maxine laughed until she snorted and hiccupped, which woke Sandy, who had curled up on the grimy floor.

"What'd I miss?" Sandy yawned, just as the antagonists of the movie were getting pelted with fruit and whatnot.

They got on a bus to the beach and slept during the ride. There was a warm breeze at the water's edge and they sprawled in the sand and dozed some more, until a few kids danced over their fully clothed bodies, singing.

"Say goodbye to the good old days!" they squealed. "Say goodbye to the good old days!"

A girl, not more than five or six, stopped and hovered her buttocks directly over Maxine's purse and farted. Maxine laughed and rolled around in the sand and the children loped off toward the breakers, peeling off their shirts as they went.

* * *

Juda exits out of the parking garage, pointing his truck toward the ramps that are usually flowing freely and not policed by hulking military carriers. He is stopped at a checkpoint. The smoke is thick and the soldier bends down to peer inside, talking to someone on his radio.

"Yessir," the soldier says and lowers his weapon and imbeds a bullet into Juda's face.

*   *   *

On the flight home, they didn't sit together. Maxine was a row up from Gail, and Sandy was far in the back, near the bathrooms. It was hard to get a button connection, and Gail finally gave up and decided to rely on the conversations around him for updates about the violent conflicts and the government upheaval. Every few minutes there would be a sigh or a groan from a nearby seat.

As they were flying over the Yukon, it was Maxine who lamented, throwing her head back in the seat.

"Oh god," she said. "Oh god."

Then it was silent all around for a while. The stewardess played a never-ending old movie, and Gail slept for the last four hours, until they skipped onto the tarmac. People grabbed their bags in silence and there were a few nervous smiles, people calling to check on cabs and rides.

"What have we made it back to?" Gail said as he stood behind her in the tunnel.

She shrugged and looked around for Sandy, who was way in the back of the line. She waved to him.

"I don't know," she said.

As they snaked through a series of barriers under a cascade of unusually rough orders and instructions from the airport loudspeakers, they noticed their line was being routed through a set of double doors. There were handmade signs taped to these doors, stating: ALL PHONES OFF!

This last passage was a brightly lit room filled with military who shouldered compact weapons. There were two men in black uniforms at the last door, on the other side of the room. Some people were being led behind screens, just to the right of this door, where they were presumably being sat to wait for some sort of reprimand or additional detainment.

"Come with me," one of the regular soldiers said as Gail and Maxine—and suddenly Sandy, who had cut his way up to stand with them—inched right up to the menacingly dressed pair. The soldier led a middle-aged woman off behind the screens. Both of the men in black each held a tablet with rows of photographs scrolling up and down the glass.

"You," the one on the left said to Gail, "go through this door and leave the airport."

The other one snapped her head at Maxine and Sandy.

"Two more," she told the regular soldier.

Gail watched wordlessly as his friends, his cohorts in chaos from China, were pushed behind the screens to god knows where, awaiting god knows what.

"I can go?" Gail asked quietly.

"Don't make me change my mind."

* * *

Gail avoided the Friday lunch crew that first week back. He said he had to catch up some, there being so many files on his desk and all that. His young colleagues smiled and said he owed them a story next week. They expected big tales from him. Nobody seemed shaken by the recent events. Everybody went around like nothing was wrong, nothing out of the ordinary.

He dropped into his chair and ran his fingers along the smooth mahogany desktop. There was one folder in his drawer and he pulled it out and opened it and spread the papers out like a fan. On each sheet there was a stapled photo, a name, a bio, and a series of instructions. For each one of his friends at the table in the atrium, he had a written mandate to observe and document them.

When it was his turn to spin his fables about the trip to China, Gail propped his shoes into an empty chair and rested his head back in his fingers. He grinned big and began a fabulous lie.

"Well, it was one of the nicest hotels in the Liwan District. Great food, spicy beer, and some of the finest beaches in the entire People's Republic."

20.

Orel and Nico shiver at first, in the darkness, an immutable stench underfoot. Orel falls to his right and feels his hand stiffen in a quagmire that is thicker than mud, and surprisingly warm.

"Christ!" he snarls as he holds the hand out so it won't touch his clothes.

"What is it? You okay?"

"It's awful," he tells Nico. "There's bags of, like, crap over here. Lots of it. Like stacked up against the wall."

Despite himself, Nico laughs. He finds a tiny flashlight in his coat and clicks it on. The beam crawls up the wall in front of them and shows nothing more than rust, chipped paint and dark stains. The lid above vibrates with wind and seems secure. The walls to the left and right are uneventful, as is the metal plate to their backs. Nico shines below and almost screams. They're standing atop sacks of filth beyond reason: Not just feces, but also rotten flesh and bones of pink and green, as endless columns of bug larvae writhe and breathe en masse.

"Mother of God," Nico whispers, his eyes bulging.

There's a garish, pulsing wad of maggots where Orel had jammed his hand. He motions for them to get out but vomits before his hand stops whirling.

They are back in the alley in seconds, breathing wildly, flinging their hands and feet to get free of larvae and waste. It only takes the pop of a rifle to bring them back into the moment. Nico ducks as a bullet ricochets above their heads, sparking against a nest of electric-wire insulators.

"Your father's late," says Nico as they watch the entry to their alley, the crumpled bodies of the man and woman still lie there. The man's face has gone gray. Orel knows what the no-show plan is, but his stomach boils with anxiety the second he starts to go over it.

"We can wait a bit, can't we?"

They know which skyrise Lucas went to. It's right around the corner. They begin the debate about whether it's best to wait or go over there and see for themselves what's going on. Nico says if they had Bixby, they could send the dog around to check things out.

"Really?" says Orel.

"No. I made that up." Nico answers with a tight smile, eyes frantic with fright.

They decide to wait a little more—maybe twenty minutes, thirty tops.

* * *

Gerard is stuck behind a slow-moving caravan of mini-buses and cattle trailers, a line of easily a hundred, all crammed with wild-eyed citoyens. They chug to a railway crossing and the red lights blink on and the arms begin to ease down. Nan is uneasy about having to wait.

"This is wasting gas too," she complains out her window, loudly. She pulls her rifle from under the seat and checks it over. "I haven't shot this thing in a couple years," she muses, turning it so she can read the lettering on the barrel. "Made in ... Hebron, Kentucky."

She turns her head along with Gerard as they watch a man wrapped in a dirty quilt scramble up the embankment to watch the passing train.

"Good old Southern weapon," she continues as the man stands on the peak and waves, like it is the old times when the presidents used to stump by railroad. "Last time I shot it was... when? Wasn't it when the dogs were still puppies and we had a bobcat at your pens?"

Gerard chews his lips and thinks hard.

"I believe it was," he says. Nan shot and killed that bobcat from fifty yards, uphill, through willows and vines, in a pouring rain. "One of the best shots I ever saw too."

She credits the Navy with teaching her how to defend herself, her family, and her property. *In that order*, she likes to say. Now she is watching the old-timer in the blanket give his greetings to a hurtling passenger train. It is one of those trains with the windows blackened-out. Even the numbers and letters that you usually see are gone. It is simply an anonymous, blind conveyance—not much different, on the surface, than a piece of pipe.

"I can still shoot a bottle from two-hundred yards," Nan boasts, a smile on her lips now.

"Could you shoot that fella's hat off his head?" he asks, pointing to the old geezer under the quilt, who is wearing some type of headdress atop a mane of snowy white hair.

"I could. You want me to?" She lifts the rifle to the dashboard and chuckles. He waves at the barrel and says for her to get it out of sight before these people get any more unnerved than they already are. The train greeter puts his hands on his hips as the last cars shoot past. You can see by the way his mouth moves that he's either talking to this train or singing.

The man turns and starts his wobbly saunter back down to the road. He walks like his knees are giving out or maybe something's wrong with his hips. Nan says he looks like an uncle she used to visit in Florida, many moons ago, who drank liquor for breakfast, lunch, and dinner.

"Drank it for snacks," she says.

As the old stranger reaches the bottom of the embankment, somebody shoots him in the neck, spinning him the way a gust of wind does a leaf. He goes down on one arm, which snaps like a twig, his forehead smacking the spot where the gravel meets the pavement.

"Yep," Gerard mutters. "Time to get back on the road now."

The crossing arms lift slowly and the caravan sputters forward. Except for one truck. This truck is orange and has hand-painted lettering on its tailgate and doors which reads: *FAITH HEALER: JONAS—FOR HIRE*. A bowlegged woman in a flowered shawl jumps out of the passenger side and, pausing between mini-buses to make sure she won't get run over, hobbles over to the train greeter who is bleeding out.

When they pass her, she is pushing some hair out of his eyes as she whispers something important into his dead ear.

* * *

A pack of soldiers carrying shields lumber up the street toward Lucas, as he breaks away from the skyrise. One block is all he has to navigate to reach the alley and the terminal. The rain has stopped again and a glow—that elusive sun—is pulsing through the cloud deck. He pushes against a brick bus stop as the phalanx stomps past him, a few helmets turning his way. He makes sure they see his old badge, the government identification.

He realizes that he is, oddly enough, dehydrated, thanks in part to Pavla's strong coffee. There is a fountain behind the stop, a few steps from the alley he used to get here from the train terminal. The water is acrid but he knows it's safe. Most likely safe. Possibly safe. There is little worry the radiation from the nuke site has reached here already, and definitely not into the water system. But the taste is puzzling. It's not how water should taste.

"Hey!" a man up the street cries. He shouts something else that Lucas can't make out. The man is leading a pair of exhausted children, both of them tugging at his coat as he hurries toward Lucas. The children are spewing thick snot from their noses and their eyes are a glowing pink. Lucas starts to back away as they rush closer.

"Hey! No!" the man calls. He passes a water bottle back and forth between the children, who are maybe eight or ten years old. He gestures at Lucas to stop and not run up that alley. "Hey, Man! Give me a break here. You see me, don't you? You see what is happening here?"

Lucas stops and peers at the man's face. The ringlet beard, the ears with cupped lobes that Sila would often say needed dangly hoops or studded skulls. The thick scarf he wears only partly hides the tattoo of a winged Zoroaster on his neck. He puts his hand to his face and there is his History Society ring.

"Lucas!" Raphael beams, thrusting his hand out and then bear-hugging his old friend. They separate and look each other up and down. Lucas turns his palms up in question.

In a burst, Raphael explains that he was snagged by the government, as a potential subversive, but that he was deemed too valuable to exile or kill. The corrupt power needs fantasies weaved, to hide its crimes—some concessions were made to spare people with needful skills. So instead of being stabbed or shot or gassed, Raphael became a Hidden. For years he's been living in forced solitude, writing one false history after another for a government he loathes. And as of this morning, soldiers pounded on doors in his building.

"They've put many of us out," Raphael tells Lucas, pushing the kids down to sit on the bus bench, as if the Number 9 for uptown is just around the corner. "I found these guys—I think they're a brother and sister—crawling out of the plaza. *Crawling.* Like bugs. Just a few hours ago, even before they started lobbing in stun bombs. These are the grenades that will knock your eyeballs out and shatter your teeth, but they won't kill you. You may as well be dead, though, if you can't see or eat. And now they are shooting—strafing is more like it. And these two crawled out after their mother was choked to death."

Lucas looks back to where the soldiers just marched away. They aren't far off. He's not sure where Raphael and the orphans came from. They just seemed to appear in the street. Pierre is gulping from the water bottle and Desiree has her hands out, pleading for a go at it.

"This is madness," Lucas says. He can't even smile about seeing his friend after all these years. Their reunion feels like it's destined to end, at any moment, with a volley from a helicopter gunship.

"Here," Raphael says as he takes the water from the boy and passes it to the sister. "Hooligans," he adds, smirking at Lucas and then pointing to a skyrise at the far end of the street. "The one that's on fire there, see it? I was up on the gazillionth floor. Watching all this happen down here like it was on TV. Had the fireplace going and was chatting on the phone with a neighbor. And then there's a knock on the door ... a bang ... a blow made by a battering ram and the door explodes into my apartment. These doors are made of steel and polymers, remember. But it just comes in and then somebody shouts for me to get out—this guy with a spacesuit on and like a flaming sword. So we cram in to the elevators and we jolt down and go out on the street like it's parade day. And then … see it burning behind you? And all this happened right after breakfast. And I'm wandering around and I find these two. Their mother was murdered by some refugee freak who got his eyes knocked out, so he just goes around choking people. Poor things."

Lucas nods and glances at the kids, who are watching him closely.

"I have to go," he tells Raphael. He stops and tries to say something else. "I have to go," he says again.

Raphael motions to the boy and the girl. He puts his finger to his lips. The wind howls through and smoke rubs along the inside wall, but soon they emerge from the alley and stand in an empty street actually lit by sunlight. The boy turns his face to the sky and smiles.

"Stop that!" the girl tells him. "You look ugly."

Lucas sees the dumpster and the two fresh corpses heaped in front of it. He can't tell who they are and runs, drawing his pistol. He goes to a knee at their side and gasps when he sees the gray faces of the man and woman—at least what is left of the man's. The woman's eyes are half open and her tongue is stuck between her yellow teeth.

Raphael is barking orders behind him, telling the children to stop rubbing their eyes so much, that it will be impossible to see the bullets coming if you have your fists digging around in your eye sockets.

Lucas sees two pairs of boots from under the dumpster, on the other side, shifting this way and that.

"Stay there!" he hisses. "Don't move!"

He turns and motions to his friend and the children to come over, into this alley, out of the gold-glowing street and into these more protective shadows. He waves frantically for them to come over.

21.

The traffic eases once they've slipped around the conflagration of the city and its teeming wild refugees. Gerard settles back into his seat and even starts to whistle. Cyril stands in the center of the low-ceilinged cabin and makes sandwiches. He spreads salty mackerel across sliced bread and then squirts each open-faced offering with mustard. Then Torrey leans over and drops a leaf of romaine on top and folds it back together. The handing-it-out part is easy: They go to the driver first, then the mother, then to the sons, according to size.

Gerard whistles a Lowcountry work song, then switches to a more lively Texas gospel number. Nan hums along and they roll through a swampy snarl of back roads where nobody lives anymore. House after house has curtains blowing through open or broken windows. Junk cars sit neglected under shelters, vultures cruise leafless treetops, and the bones of a cow or two jut like white spears in the middle of lifeless fields.

"You know this is where the sea foam was," Gerard says as they pass a dry lakebed where a lone man, no bigger than a nail out on the moonscape, is walking with a bony dog. The *sea foam* was the first toxic sprawl into public water supply on the East Coast. Tens of thousands died, almost overnight, before anyone knew what was hitting them.

"Lucas told me about it," he goes on as Nan squints because the sun—a lonesome guest in this world—sparkles through these low dark clouds. "He said nobody to this day really knows what caused it."

"But they know what happened because of it," she grumbles. Nan is no friend to the government. They still send her checks from her time in the Navy and she cashes them, saying it is what they owe everybody, not just her.

They slow down through a grove of dead Blackjack oaks, massive trees with sprawling crowns that shroud one another. Gerard says he wishes Nico were here to take a picture of it.

Haw   173

He says it is a scene like you would witness in the horror
stories of old writers. He shudders and steps back on the gas.

"Too much of anything," he says, "can be a bad thing.
But sometimes a little bit of a bad thing ..."

Gerard wags his head. He looks at Nan.

"I don't know," he says. "I've lost my train of thought."

They decide to risk a stop right inside the Virginia line. Gerard
finds an abandoned country store with a loop driveway, gravel,
weeds, and rusty pumps close by. The dog has been dancing in
circles for miles and Cyril agrees to take Bixby for a quick walk.

Nan estimates they are a hundred-fifty miles from home.
Gerard checks the dashboard numbers.

"You're off by only four miles," he tells her.

Everybody gets out and stretches their legs. Bixby
bounces off into the weeds, barking. The sun is disappearing as
a misty breeze kicks in and thunder rumbles off to the east.
Torrey kicks at one of the tires and tilts his head in thought.

"Are we going anywhere that's safer or cleaner than
where we were?" he asks. "Is it going to be better or worse
than what we had at home?"

Gerard takes a look around, hands on his hips. He tilts his
trucker hat back and spits.

"Better," he replies.

"Are you sure, Dad?"

"Pretty sure. A hundred percent sure. Positive." He looks at
Nan, who is gazing off after Cyril and Bixby. She can hear them,
but they're hidden behind some brambles beside the store.

"It's going to be better, Honey," she tells her youngest.
"Me and your dad can't really tell you how it's going to be
better, or how much it will be, but it is going to be a big
improvement for us. You wait and see, Son. A big
improvement all around."

It doesn't take long for Bixby to come scooting back out
of the crackly weeds. He waits for Cyril to follow, and then
makes a complete run around the truck, barking again. He
stops cold when thunder shakes the earth, growing closer.

"Let's hit it," Gerard says, "before it hits us."

* * *

The red dot shines, like a pilot light keeps vigil for a blooming gas, and then it starts to spread. It becomes enormous circles, the rings of a new sun, evacuating all available sources of dilation. It crushes upon the Word of God and obliterates all awareness of divinity, infallibility, salvation, remorse, even as it forgets itself and becomes new impossible things.

The walls of the reactor fragment, blow as though a celestial wind has cleansed the scorched earth, returned time to its first ticks in a new clock, better than the one before.

* * *

Lucas is watching when Raphael scoops up the boy and girl and sprints for the alley. He's staring right at the old dear friend when a sizzling wave of shells mushrooms out the other sides of their bodies, skittering far down the street like breaking glass. The man-and-children mass collapses on the sidewalk, the girl tumbling and rolling. Her gasping lungs sputter blood as she tries to get up and run again. She takes one lunging step and then her eyes roll back and she falls atop the man/woman aggregate marking the entrance to this alley for an hour.

Raphael clutches the boy to his breast, his lips parted in a weird smile and his eyes wide open and calm—dead. The boy whimpers a bit until a new shower of bullets rains down, pocking the street, walls, and even the granite slabs along the curbing, silencing him.

Lucas signals for his boys to run. He screams it will only take seconds to round the corner and be into the terminal.

"Go straight for the gate!" he bellows as they flash past. "Northbound train … the express!"

The gunship overhead is flooding the plaza with fire now, crushing them. Lucas sprints, staying hunched, and goes sliding into the stairwell, catches himself and leaps several steps at a time until he is at the bottom. He runs with others toward the Acela platform, everybody shouting names of loved ones.

He grabs Orel by the elbow and spins him around.

"Here," he gasps, "this bag—inside of it, your mother is here. Take it with you."

He hugs his son in a squeeze and kisses his hair.

"Do good," he says.

22.

They took one trip not long after the fire that took Sila, with the liturgies and ceremony of death still fresh in their minds. Orel had just gotten a book for his birthday, a children's book with animated red lions and giant, sweet, shadowy clouds that followed the protagonists around, musical trees, and lobsters that played angelic harps. The father read it every night at bedtime.

They packed this book and took it with them on their trip to an island getaway (of sorts) on the coast. Their cottage was small, a cedar shake with lime trim and no screens in the windows. The breakers would murmur all day and night, whispering through the sea oats and lacquering their vague sunburns with a scent neither sweet nor sour.

Lucas took the boy fishing in a lagoon on the opposite side of the island, where the freshwater transuded and would, at night, sweep in spot and croaker fish. They would stand their poles in plastic tubes, a sort of parade rest effect, and crawl under a wide umbrella and rehash this fable of red lions, knowledgeable nebulae, and crustaceans with orchestral abilities.

Every so often the tip of a pole would dance lightly and they would spring into action, sand flying, the book smacking closed and flung onto their towels. It was always a hoax, a sham as Lucas called it, and never a fish on the line. So in the late afternoons they would tramp along the firm wet sand of the tideline and go to the closest fish shack and pick out their own. Snapper, red drum, black bass and flounder—not to mention the shrimp and oysters and crabmeat they would haul back to drizzle with butter and hot sauce.

They found a dying sea turtle on their third night and sat in the cool white sand and reflected for a while. There was a soft wind from the ocean and it was nice, quiet enough without being too quiet. Orel kept a shaky beam of light on the sluggish loggerhead. The turtle acted like it could not stop yawning, which Lucas explained was its way of gasping for breath.

Its protuberant eyes were glazed with discharge and it stared blindly at distant dunes. One of its flippers wiped listlessly at imaginary currents. Its shell was coated with sickly pale fibers, and whenever the breeze stilled it put out an odor like spoiled greens.

"We have to let it die in private," Lucas told his son. He said it was an honor system that sea creatures valued. Beyond all other codes, this one was their most revered.

They came back the next morning to find the loggerhead gone. There had been a storm during the night, brief and violent. Shells were everywhere and kelp and wracks littered the shore. The boy became distracted with the mess and forgot his sadness over the turtle. That evening they nestled into the rattan sofa and Lucas read from the book as a new storm drifted in off the Atlantic.

"Why were people afraid of thunder and lightning?" asked Orel.

His father explained that it was uncommon before to have daily squalls and tempests. It is like now, when people don't get excited when it snows.

"I like the snow," the boy said.

"You won't always."

"I know I will."

"Maybe you will and maybe you won't."

"What happened to that turtle?"

"He died."

The boy fell silent. You could feel his questions sliding through his body, from his chest into his head—swirling there in doubt and confusion—and then back down through the shoulders into his arms, where they took shape in tiny patterns he traced on the sofa cushions. He seemed to be drawing faces—both smiley and frowny.

It was the Fourth of July that last full day, Friday. The sun peered down on the coast and a few lithe teenage girls even peeled down to their bikinis and stretched out in the sand. Lucas sat on their tiny deck and watched people dip only to their knees in the water, toss balls and Frisbees, dig craters in the sand, and let grinning goofy dads plop in to be buried up to their necks and ankles.

"I don't want you to die," the boy said quietly after a while.

He sat on the bench beside his father and rested his head against his dad's arm.

Suddenly there was a whooshing rocket with a pink tail, shot from a pier down the shore. The boy gasped a little and squeezed his father's hand. He said he wanted them to do that. Wasn't that what people did before, like when Daddy was a boy, on the Fourth of July?

"Let me get my wallet," Lucas said.

At dusk they went onto the deck and climbed the narrow ladder up to the roof of the cottage and onto a crow's nest no wider than a shower stall. Lucas helped his son onto the railing and they lit bottle rockets and roman candles until they were all out. Down along the beach there were pockets of families, some vacationing and some not, shooting fireworks into the dark sky. After a while they looked up and saw that stars were out, abundant and shiny.

Orel asked what a shooting star was and Lucas told him.

"Have you ever seen one?" the boy asked.

"No."

"Oh. But I hope you do someday, Daddy."

Later, they read the book again, watched the dazzling animated displays they had seen a hundred times by now—and they laughed at each joke as if for the first time. The young lobster set his mind to play Bach on the harp by the end of the fall semester. And he did it. Just in time for the school's winter play. Orel fell asleep as the lobster flicked away at one of the concertos.

That night, Lucas kept the windows open, so they could smell the last hours of sand and sea. They packed and had a little breakfast at a diner near the train station. The boy ate his eggs and pancakes with the usual enthusiasm, while the father drooped over his coffee and toast and let the newspaper at his elbow go unread.

On the train, the boy stuck his finger in the man's ribs to get his attention. He looked up with his bright eyes and put his face in its most serious position.

"It's okay if you die," Orel said. "I just want you to wait till I'm grown."

"I'll do what I can."

"And I mean grown. Not just in sixth grade or something. I mean grown into a full-sized man."

Lucas smiled and pinched the boy's freckly cheek.

"You're practically there already," he told his son.

* * *

Gail looks at his button and sees the last train is soon to board. He has come out the shipping exit, where great slabs of concrete are stained from years of toil and secrete brown sweat from these infinite rains. He notices the exhaust fans have stopped. Then a message glows on his screen. The missing scientist is located.

Gail reaches out to another of his agents, a woman who prowls the train depot.

Westward there is a scalding red eye that shivers in its own gory nightmare. He hears the whistle of the last train arriving, the final note of a fugue.

* * *

The boys are on the train, shoving away panicked exiles that have not slept in days. Orel grabs his bag from an old man who is being dragged away from the doors, bellowing about some wicked monster who suffocates little children in their sleep. Nico kicks at the lunatic to get him off of Orel.

Lucas is tossed around on the platform, wrenching his way through a knot of wailing dirty women in rags. He is two feet from the door. One of the women receives a buzz on her government-issued button, an order from Gail. She clutches her knife.

"Repent!" someone shouts, and gunfire erupts back by the turnstiles. People hit the deck in waves, leaving others to simply cover their heads with their hands. The woman with the knife turns to Lucas and bares her teeth, squatting next to him like an animal, some sort of red scarf wrapped around her dreadlocks. She lunges and stabs him in the neck, then in the heart. And then she moves on, leaping over still-prostrate bodies, as the doors to the train clamp shut and the engineer rolls the last whistle for his departing express to the North.

Orel is frantic. He sees his father slumped on his knees, head bowed. The woman in the red head wrap is bounding away into a crowd while someone shoots wildly. He smacks the glass and calls out. He pounds the window with the heel of his hand and screams his father's name. He tries to dislodge the pane and get his father's attention, who remains kneeling as if in prayer. He pulls out his pistol and points it at the glass and fires—but only cracks it, sending the car into mayhem.

A big bearded man in work clothes bear-hugs Orel and wrestles the gun away, cursing at him for nearly killing someone, including himself.

"Look at that," the man says in a baritone, pointing at the spidery window which is glowing a shade of crimson. "My god, look at what's happening back there."

Red smoke engulfs the receding platform just as the sky itself seems to bleed, as when a throat is slashed. Orel and Nico watch as the city fades, violently and charred.

* * *

Gail enters the platform and watches the spectacle, what he can see through the char. The dying, as they writhe, are reciting doxologies, demanding swift and peaceful death. He steps over a decapitated child and goes where he can look up the tracks, then down.

It reminds him of a day on the killing floors at the farm, years and years before.

"We can bring the mountains underfoot," he sings lightly, to nobody, a song his grandfather used to sing, "and build our kingdom here. But what goes where the mountains were? What of the void left by that, my dear?"

* * *

The train rumbles between spiky black pines at a jarring speed. Some of the passengers are sobbing and others, like Orel, are staring out of windows, mute as stones. Nico touches his arm, but Orel does not react. They shoot around a bend, cross a concrete bridge into a town that is engulfed in white smoke. Then they are belched into a clearing, the windows momentarily frosting with white ash, before the wind sweeps it away. There are bodies scattered in the distance, as if thrown about a barren waste by a god, or a demon, in a rage over their deaths. Orel looks at the cracked glass, where he tried to shoot out the window to get to his father. Nico follows his gaze.

"None of the air can get in here," Nico says. "We're going too fast."

"It's poison, isn't it?" Orel says. "The air is poisonous."

Nico nods. He looks around the train car, sees that other passengers are watching the carnage scroll past. At one point there is a man doubled over a fence, then a girl sprawled just on the other side. Somebody in the back of the car asks if anyone knows where the train is heading. Nico reaches out, takes Orel's hand, and squeezes it. He turns around.

"North," he says. He takes out his button with his free hand and sees a message from Nan. His mother says they are safe in Virginia, back on the highway heading north at a fast clip. She prays that he is able to read this.

"They've made it," he says, softly, to Orel. They go back to watching the scenes out the window, the murky world that slowly comes back to life. First, there is a little bird on a wire, and then a larger one, a crow, in flight. As they cross a sluggish river which is just a blur, Orel's head snaps to see something.

"Turtle," he says. "I think I saw a turtle."

Soon they are slowing, and the ceiling lights glow on—a sign they will soon stop. Nico checks his button to get their location. Somebody a few rows ahead beats him to it, calling out that they are just outside of Richmond. Nico checks to see if Orel understands what is happening, and sees the shock of his father's death still has a white grip on him. He gives Orel's arm a squeeze.

"I'm here," Nico says.

Orel nods. He tries to smile. He picks up the bag from between his feet and opens it. There is money in a box and there, wrapped in felt, is his mother. For the first time in years, he touches her.

More books from
Harvard Square Editions: